Apache Gold

by

Earl Farabaugh

DORRANCE PUBLISHING CO
EST. 1920
PITTSBURGH, PENNSYLVANIA 15238

The contents of this work, including, but not limited to, the accuracy of events, people, and places depicted; opinions expressed; permission to use previously published materials included; and any advice given or actions advocated are solely the responsibility of the author, who assumes all liability for said work and indemnifies the publisher against any claims stemming from publication of the work.

All Rights Reserved
Copyright © 2021 by Earl Farabaugh

No part of this book may be reproduced or transmitted, downloaded, distributed, reverse engineered, or stored in or introduced into any information storage and retrieval system, in any form or by any means, including photocopying and recording, whether electronic or mechanical, now known or hereinafter invented without permission in writing from the publisher.

Dorrance Publishing Co
585 Alpha Drive
Pittsburgh, PA 15238
Visit our website at *www.dorrancebookstore.com*

ISBN: 978-1-6495-7253-0
eISBN: 978-1-6495-7761-0

Table of Contents

Prologue – Arizona territory 1841 vii
Chapter 1 1
Chapter 2 5
Chapter 3 11
Chapter 4 17
Chapter 5 23
Chapter 6 35
Chapter 7 43
Chapter 8 49
Chapter 9 59
Chapter 10 65
Chapter 11 69
Chapter 12 81
Chapter 13 89
Chapter 14 91
Chapter 15 97
Chapter 16 103
Chapter 17 109
Chapter 18 131
Chapter 19 137
Chapter 20 147
Chapter 21 155
Chapter 22 161
Chapter 23 165

Prologue – Arizona Territory 1841

The column of dust could be seen miles away. Eyes narrowed in the blistering sunlight to focus on the intruders. The Apache were sole owners of the Superstition Mountains. Their gods lived among the tall peaks and severe canyons. The line of wagons and mules kept coming from the South. Mexico had invaded their lands before but was turned away.

Miguel Peralta directed the wagons to spread out to keep the dust plumes from choking the mules. The Peraltas were a wealthy family from northern Mexico. This would be the last foray into the Arizona territory for gold. The opportunities to mine in this area would be nil in the future. Miguel had brought with him a large party of almost seventy-five miners, smelters and general laborers. Looking at maps made years earlier gave a general description of likely places to mine.

Miguel was familiar with the Mescalero Apache culture. He wanted no part of having to defend his group against them. The Zuni Indians called these people "Apachu," meaning enemy. In their own dialects, the Apache referred to themselves as "the people" in their language, "Tinneh" or "Tinde." Apache Indians had several different tribes or clans, Chiricahua, Western Apache, Mescalero, Jicarilla, Lipan and Kiowa. Because of their nomadic culture, a group of Apaches could be associated with more than one tribe.

This would be the last time Peralta would be searching for gold this far north. The costs involved and the lives put at risk were a major factor. The leaders in Mexico City were having difficulties with the United States and the Texas territory wanted to cede from Mexico and become an independent nation. The Peralta gold would go a long way to pay for an army to defend the land. Miguel was hoping that this gold would win him the ambassador post to Spain after all this was finished.

Miguel had calculated that about another week or so, of travel before the caravan would reach the gold rich lands near Superstition Mountains. His Indian scouts had made some contact with a few small bands of Apache along the way. They bartered with the Apaches and in the exchange the miners acquired four Indian women as slaves. It seems that the Apaches would attack neighboring villages and steal the food and women. The captured women were regarded as slaves, a commodity to be traded. Miguel found these women to be an asset to his expedition as they could do the mundane chores of cooking and keeping the camp clean.

From a mountain peak some miles distant, two Apache Indians watched the slow caravan wind its way toward the mountains. The older Apache, named Black Coyote (dilhil ba'ts'ote'), thought it odd for anyone to be moving in the heat of the day. He and Two Dogs (naki hó shé), the younger warrior, would circle around to get a better look.

Apache men were thin and not very tall. They had developed superior stamina from their times on the plains. It was said that an Apache warrior could cover almost 50 miles in a day on foot. The fighting spirit and physical conditioning made the Apache warrior, no matter which tribe, a formidable enemy. When horses were introduced into the country, by the Spanish, Indians from all tribes adapted well and became excellent horsemen. The horse extended the range of each settlement and changed the Indian methods of war.

The Peralta caravan was making way through the Sonoran Desert. Many different kinds of vegetation live in this desert. Most noticeable is the saguaro cactus. The main trunk of the saguaro with limbs reaching out and skyward as if to say "I give up." Saguaros can be quite old. It's said that the arms of the cactus don't grow until the cactus is over 50 years old. A red fruit develops from the flowers that bloom in springtime. With the capacity to hold large amounts of water, the saguaro cactus can sustain life in the desert. Mesquite is plentiful in the desert. It's a tree with twisted trunk and limbs. The seed pods are edible and the wood is dense and burns with a high heat.

The two Indians came close to the caravan and watched as the wagons lumbered past with several teams of mules pulling each wagon. Some men were on horseback but they stayed close to the column. Black Coyote crouched between two large rocks and saw the men on the wagons wearing large brimmed hats. He had seen the large hats before and now knew the caravan was from the land South of the desert. He watched quietly until the stream of men and wagons had passed and were some distance ahead.

It took two days for Black Coyote and Two Dogs to make it back to the camp. That night a meeting with the elders was held and Black Coyote told of the things he saw. Many wondered what this meant. One thing that Black Coyote observed was, a few men carried the long guns and there were some Indian women and men in the wagon train. Many opinions were offered and each discussed. The elders finally settled that this was not a war party but to watch closely the men with the large hats.

The caravan reached the foothills of the Superstition Mountains in a week. Miguel Peralta studied his maps and settled camp outside what today would be the town of Apache Junction, Arizona. The men started to excavate the dirt and a small smelter was set up to refine the gold when they came upon it. The plentiful mesquite was harvested to make charcoal as it would increase the temperatures of the fires.

The Apaches watched the camp from afar. They saw the land being dug up and huge piles of dirt building from the excavations. The elders decided to have parley with the intruders. The Apache women from the camp went to a small stream for water each morning. It was here that the warriors made known their wishes and bid the women to tell the chief of this expedition their desires to talk. A place of prominence was selected and Miguel Peralta came with a couple of his Indian scouts to act as interpreters and some men a few steps away with muskets at the ready.

Two elders stood with several braves around them. The elders let it be known to the Mescalero Indian interpreters that this place and the whole of the Superstition Mountains were sacred to the Western Apache clans. The digging and piling of rocks and dirt about was a desecration to the gods that resided within the mountains. The elders said that if the men with the large hats would travel ten days to the sunset, they would be able to dig holes and no one would mind.

   Miguel Peralta smiled when his scouts relayed the message. He looked at the weapons the Indians brandished. Bows and arrows, lances, and large clubs seemed to be the whole of the Indian intimidation. He motioned to his men with the muskets to take two steps forward and hold their muskets out. The elders didn't need any interpreter to tell them that the man with the black hair under his nose didn't think much of this parley. Without emotion the Apaches withdrew from the site. Miguel was pleased with himself as he walked back to the camp but he knew this issue wasn't over. He would have to post guards and keep sentries throughout the day. The Apache Indians were not noted for any activity at night. This would pull some abled bodied men from the mining.

   As time went on, the piles of tailings grew and the smelter was kept busy day and night. Men had scoured the hills for more mesquite and any wild game. They occasionally found a small antelope to augment the stores. Most of the meat was smoked and dried. This kept the meat longer and it was a flavoring for the stews that the Indian women learned to prepare. The women would take large pottery jars to the small stream to clean and bring water back to the camp. Miguel had sentries to watch the women and oversee their activities when not in camp.

   One of the slave women, Yellow Cat (litsog gidi), was collecting water in a jug one day and saw that she was watched not only by the sentry with a large hat, but concealed in the heavy brush, an Apache warrior. After a couple days, she returned to the stream and the same warrior was there. The sentry was not paying much attention and she was able to talk with the Indian. He wanted to know how many guns there were in the camp and if there was any attempt to make permanent structures. He told her he would be watching her to see when she came to the stream and await her answer. Yellow Cat looked to see if the sentry was suspicious of anything but he was smoking something in a handmade pipe. As she turned to look at the warrior, he had vanished without a sound. As Yellow Cat returned to the encampment, she thought of what happened and was a bit relieved to know that her people were watching.

She had been captive to the men with large hats for some time and was sure they wanted to have their way with her. The man with the hair under his nose told all of the workers, that the women were not to be touched by any of the men. He bought them and they were his property. Yellow Cat was thin for her age. She was almost 30 as the seasons were measured. She kept her black hair braided and the dress was made of cougar skin that had been scraped, tanned, and stitched together with the tendons from the same cat. She had the usual high cheekbones but an unusual mark on her chin was a cleft that no other Indian she knew ever had. Many stories were made up to explain this mark.

Yellow Cat had wandered the camp and made mental notes of the long guns and the ones that were on a belt. She had counted on her hand three times, the long guns and two hands plus two of guns on belts. There weren't any structures other than the wagons and tents. It was two days before her next trip to the stream. as she approached the stream with jugs, she looked carefully and saw a moccasin under some heavy brush. The sentry took his post on some rocks to look out over the barranca. Yellow Cat on hands and knees went about her business of washing the jugs and quietly relayed her findings to the hidden warrior. She turned to go with the containers of water and she saw that the moccasin was gone. A slight smile came across her face as she continued up the path.

The Peralta mining expedition had been working for almost a year. The smelted gold was piling up in a tent that was guarded closely. Miguel calculated that if mules could carry almost three hundred pounds of gold, he would need almost forty mules to carry the treasure. Some wagons would have to be left behind. But the retreat back into Mexico would be faster than the trek out.

The scouts would have to stay till they all crossed into Sonora Mexico. Miguel Peralta wanted to finish his trek and arrive in Cananea Mexico. Cananea was an Apache word for horsemeat. But to Miguel Peralta, the gold and silver that had been discovered at Cananea in the 1700s had played out and the mines were abandoned. Little did Miguel know, the now useless land was a site of immense copper ore. Centuries later it was destined to become one of the largest open pit copper mines in the world. If the expedition could manage ten miles a day, it would be about three weeks to reach their destination.

The women and other Apache Indians collected the bladders and stomachs of large game that had been killed for meat. The membranes were tanned and stretched. Finally, they were hand sewn together. They could carry two to four gallons of water. Well-watered animals were not likely to stampede in the direction of sparse watering holes. Miguel thought he had accounted for everything. The smoked meat was rationed to build up the supply for the journey home. The smelting process was almost finished.

Huge piles of tailings littered the campsite. Miguel thought about these telltale signs of human activity. If there ever was a chance to come back and claim anymore of the gold, these mounds were a dead giveaway of mining potentials. Only thing to do was to return this waste back to the mining areas and cover them with brush and transplant some of the cactus and other weeds. The smelters were placed in the holes in the ground along with the mining picks and shovels. No need to take them back. Indians watched the replacement of the heaps of dirt back to the places that had initially been removed. These men with the large hats provided the elder councils with much to talk about.

Yellow Cat came to the stream more often these last days and she told the hidden warrior that she thought the camp was getting ready to leave soon. The provisions were being amassed on three wagons and many wooden packs were made for the mules to carry. She was fearful that when this ended, the men with the large hats would kill the women. She could not see what useful purpose was needed for the women other than provide for the pleasures of the men.

Elders of the Western Apache clan met with other Apache clans more distant and told them of the sacrilege that was being done to their mountains. It was not often the different clans combine to face a threat. But this time, the desecration of the mountains was a bond that all clans could understand. The elders knew that the long guns were weapons that they could not defeat. A plan had to be devised that would render the guns useless.

After much discussion, they thought that some kind of ambush with the element of surprise to be the best way to overcome the range of the long guns. It would have to be overwhelming numbers to offset. One of the elders, Big Owl (búh nchaa), suggested that an ambush in a canyon with no way out would be correct. If smaller band of warriors could chase the men with the big hats into the canyon, a large assembly of warriors could rain arrows down from hiding places from above. This was discussed by many of the clans. They all agreed to do this but the question of when had to be answered.

Two Dogs said that he had been watching and talking with a slave woman who came to collect water. She told him that the mules were being fitted with large bags to carry their yellow metal. Some wagons were being taken apart to scavenge the wood. He said that the men with large hats were putting the soil back into the holes they dug. This had many in the council confused. Dig a hole for weeks and then put the dirt back. The mules would be loaded with a lot of weight and perhaps they could stampede the mules with fire. The men with large hats would go after the mules and could be easily killed while distracted.

It was agreed by all of the clan elders that this would be the plan and the warriors would have to kill everyone. Someone said that it wasn't right to kill the women in the group as they were slaves and had provided useful information. It was decided that the women would be spared if possible and the Apache men who were interpreters were to be killed along with the men with large hats. The additional warriors from the other clans were to stay close. No one was to make any attempt to contact the miners or let the miners know there were over four hundred warriors waiting to attack.

The last day began like all the others. Sky was a cloudless blue, and the sun mercilessly hot. The tents that were left were taken down and wagons of food and water loaded. Miguel surveyed the work and felt that this undertaking would be a fine accomplishment to his family. The workers now led the mules to make four columns and the wagons took the rear of the convoy. Miguel had the women slaves brought to him along with an Apache interpreter. The women were to load the water bladders on to the last wagon. He instructed the Indian women to make ready to strike camp and to follow behind the caravan.

The Apache Indians made numerous piles of mesquite wood along the trail that the Mexicans had come. The piles were arranged such that when lit, the caravan would have to move to the West. This would direct them into a box canyon and there would be no way out. It was here that most of the Indians would hide, waiting to ambush the miners.

It took some time to get the entire caravan moving and it was by noon that all of the mules loaded with the gold were moving down the trail. Miguel supervised the miners from the middle of the caravan. He was quite pleased with how this expedition had completed its objectives. He counted 34 mules each loaded with approximately 300 pounds of smelted gold. He smiled to himself, thinking of all the possibilities this would present to his family.

The caravan had proceeded several miles from its camp. Apache Indians lay in wait to set fire to several piles of dried mesquite when the time was ripe. Miguel noticed the piles of wood and wondered to himself why he hadn't seen these on the way into the campsite. When the time was right, several of the piles were lit, sending hot flames and smoke skyward along the length of the caravan. The horses and loaded mules attempted to get away from the smoke and flames throwing the miners from horseback and running helter-skelter. The Apaches plan worked to perfection. The horses ran into the canyon to escape the flames, miners running furiously after them. The miner's fate was sealed.

Arrows rained down on them and they had no opportunity to defend themselves. Because the water wagon was so slow, and almost a mile behind the wagon train, it was not affected by the fires. The Indian women were spared being part of the massacre.

The Apache Indians inspected their hapless victims and made sure that none survived. They collected the horses but were undecided what to do with the mules loaded with the yellow metal. Some suggested that the yellow metal be returned to the holes the miners had dug. Others wanted to let it lie and eat the mules. They finally came upon the water wagon with the Indian women on board. Yellow Cat and the other women were escorted to the Apache camp. In the end, the gold laden mules were stampeded into the desert. The mules laden with the heavy sacks galloped over the barren land. The stampede of mules ran over a cliff and the animals fell to their death several hundred feet below. There would be a pile of bones and bags of gold littering the bottom of the cliff. It would take a bit of time, but the vultures and coyotes would feast on the remains.

Chapter 1

The buzzer went off and there was no sign of daylight. Jack opened one eye and surveyed the darkness. Slowly he pulled his feet onto the floor and waited for his senses to catch up. It was six-thirty and the regimen started the same most every day during the work week. He pulled on the grey sweats, socks and his running shoes. Jack was out of the apartment and jogging hard to the high school track inside of ten minutes. He'd do forty minutes of hard jogging and back to the apartment to shower and dress for work.

    This had been his routine for almost five years. The doctor told him tests showed his cholesterol too high for a man in his late thirties. Jack Cummings was about six foot and his weight stayed around one eighty-five. He took great store in the cautions of the health professions. Jack worked as an actuary for a major insurance firm in Chicago. It wouldn't do for an insurance man to suffer the same ills as the masses that he insured.

Jack's apartment was rather Spartan but impeccably neat. This was a direct reflection of his personality, neat, ordered, and very methodical. A first impression upon entering this single man's apartment is that he has a maid. His pleasant way and neatness didn't interfere in his relationships with others. He picked a dark suit to match the somber overcast weather. Chicago had some of the nastiest weather and today was a forecast of things to come. The joke was told that the word "Chicago" in the Illinois Indian language meant, "crappy swampland."

He'd been at this particular job since his master's degree some eight years ago. As he inspected the knotted tie in the mirror, he thought about doing something different with his life. But the pay was good here and most people at the company left the statisticians, actuaries and anyone with a head for mathematics to themselves. One last look around, bed already made, towels hung perfectly and nothing in the sink. Time to join the masses wedging their way into Chicago's downtown. The office was filling up and folks were at various cubicles with coffee and something to munch on. Jack had an office that was away from the herd. His desk reflected the continuation of the preciseness of his apartment. While there were volumes of reports and statistical data, everything had a place. The only break from the official company desk was a five by seven picture of Sylvia, his latest flame. She photographed well. Sylvia was a strawberry blonde with green eyes. Although the picture didn't show it, she was five foot eight inches tall and thin build. Sylvia worked as an assistant city manager for the city of Joliet. Jack told Sylvia that she was the eye candy that was needed when the administration needed to explain their latest mistake. Sylvia laughed and shook her long hair.

She said that she had good job security then. Although Jack and Sylvia had some very intense passions, neither was ready for marriage.

Bill Harding came down the hall with an arm load of computer printout. Bill was a balding man in his late 50s. His pace was rather swift and determined and was headed straight for Jack's office. Jack knew that when Bill was headed to his office, there was a problem that needed to be unraveled.

"Jack, I hate to put this on your desk, but there is a data problem with our office in Atlanta. The runs they made set an asset valuation that is too low to smooth the effects of short-term volatility in the market value of assets."

"Sorry to hear that, Bill; I guess I'll have to take a look at the value of the pension plan investments and any other property." Jack knew that there was nothing wrong with the code. He suspected that the turnover in personnel the last few months may have had something to do with this change.

"I'll give a call to Atlanta and see if I can dig anything up." Jack was hoping that this would be enough to placate Bill. It wasn't anything major and Jack had lots of time on his hands. Bill seemed relieved that Jack would've taken this task on without any argument. Jack thought to himself if the phone call doesn't work, then a trip to Atlanta was required. Just don't smile while Bill is in the room. The rest of the day consisted of some standard runs and two charts for the eight o'clock meeting the next day.

Chapter 2

"Each of you grab a leg. Make sure the hooves are facing down and pull until you see the head and neck come out. When Mama is ready to make another push, you have to get the torso all the way out or her vaginal walls may bruise or crush a rib. The rest will come out in sort of a gush and be very easy."

Maria Two Crows (nakih gaage´) was very experienced with birthing of large animals. She saw her grandfather do this when she was very small. The veterinarian, Dr. Mitchell, gave her many lessons on how to handle animals and their ills. She was almost as good as the vet. Her grandfather told her that most large animals give birth to only one. He said it was nature's way of making sure that the young would get enough milk and attention of mother. The process was very much the same no matter the animal. When Maria asked about rabbits and their birth rate, grandfather just smiled. Maria looked on as the new foal was born. It was a dark brown male with a white diamond on its forehead. She took a little time to enjoy being a part of the life-giving process. She stopped by her grandfather's adobe house before returning to town.

Maria was full-blooded Apache Indian. She was born on the San Carlos reservation east of Phoenix Arizona. Her black hair and high cheekbones were the ancestral mark, but she had a deep cleft in her chin. Her mother had the same cleft and it was told that all the women in her family had that mark. When she was little, people would make up stories on how the cleft came to be. Most of her education was on the reservation. When Maria was about 10 years old, both of her parents died in an auto accident on the highway going into Mesa Arizona. Her lone surviving relative was her grandfather, and she stayed with him.

There was an air of despair by all the people who inhabited the reservation. The land was red and desolate. Rain rarely fell here. Only saguaro cactus, mesquite, and sage brush would defy the red clay. Strewn about the settlement were occasional old cars left as monuments to gather dust. Adobe huts would be clustered together to make various settlements throughout the reservation. This was Maria Two Crows classroom and life. She was steeped in the Apache traditions and culture and as she grew older, Maria was looking for her chance to escape.

The Apache Indians had been a nomadic people. For centuries they roamed the flatlands of Middle America. The Apache hunted buffalo along with the other tribes that lived on the plains. Although short in stature, the Apache developed an endurance and stamina far beyond most other native tribes. Gradually the encroachment of other tribes forced the Apache to seek new lands. They adapted to the severe heat of the southwest. It is interesting to note that despite the fierceness of the Apache warrior, Apache home life and culture is dominated by the female, that is, it was matriarchal.

The wedding ceremony for Apache couples was a simple ceremony. The husband had the additional duties of providing meat for his wife's parents. So, the skill of an Apache as a hunter is something that is sought after by Apache women. The women took care of most of the domestic chores including: tending to the children, keeping the fire, making meals, getting water, building wickiups, and working any animal skins that may be intended as clothing.

Coming-of-age ceremonies for young girls were known to have lasted for three or four days. On the first day of her celebration, Maria had to run to the winds. She would run in each of the four directions. Each direction was approximately five miles in length. There would be small dolls placed along the path. As she ran, she would collect the dolls and return to the village, deposit the dolls in a basket and run off in another direction. The dolls would tell how far she ran. She would start at sunup and had to conclude all four directions by sundown. On another day, she would wear a beautiful doeskin costume. She would be anointed by an elder of the clan with pollen to bless her with fertility. She would sing and dance through her duties and chores.

At the conclusion of the ceremonies, the young girls and some of the females of the families would enter into a sweat lodge. All of the women would enter a wickiup and disrobe. Inside a pile of hot rocks would have scented water poured on them to create steam. Sometimes the water would contain an extract of the peyote cactus, inducing altered mental states. The women would engage in singing, chanting and often dancing. The wickiup was guarded outside by the husbands and fathers of the women. The United States government frowned on these festivities as being drug parties and banned the performance of them. The Indians got around this restriction by performing the festivities on July 4th and telling the Indian agents they were celebrating the American independence. It was during this celebration that Maria became overcome with the peyote in the steam. She lay down, her head swimming with vague pictures of naked women dancing. A slightly pungent odor filled her lungs and she had a vision of two huge crows peering at her through the opening at the top of the wickiup. She remembered them gazing down at her, their eyes unblinking. The drug induced trance freed Maria's inhibitions. She got up and danced with the other women, her hands over her head clapping to a beat. There was a ceremonial corn dance that the Apache women performed at harvest. Maria performed the corn dance to honor the crows in her vision. In the Apache lore, crows were considered a lucky and resourceful omen. They fed on different grains and the flesh of dead animals. Later, Maria adopted the name Two Crows. Occasionally, she would have dreams of her flying as a crow throughout the reservation.

Maria's grandfather gave her every opportunity to participate in the Apache culture and ceremonies. Her core religious beliefs were of a supreme great spirit who ruled over lesser spirits and all of creation. Many stories were told about the different lesser spirits and their interaction with the Apache people. These stories were handed down from generation to generation and sometimes these tales had song and dance for emphasis. It is the Apache belief that all living things possess a spirit that comes from the one Great Spirit. Maria wasn't aware, but this religious philosophy was almost universal throughout the different tribes across North America.

She was a waitress in a small diner in Tempe Arizona. Maria only worked three days a week but this seemed sufficient to pay her bills. She worked as a volunteer part-time, in a small museum dedicated to preserving the Apache culture. The museum had various artifacts showing how the Apache culture survived the previous 400 years. Not much had changed until the white man came. There had been no need to change. The wants and needs of the culture were satisfied by the land. From the time Maria was a young girl she was mentored by an older white man who came to the reservation. He was a veterinarian who came almost every week to help the Apache men tend to their herds of livestock. If there was a procedure that was required, or a medicine to be administered, Dr. Ezra Mitchell would take extra time to show Maria what had to be done and what precautions were required.

Maria left home when she was just over 18 years of age. After a couple of months, Maria's boyfriend Billy Watson convinced her to let him move into her small apartment. Billy Watson was a young man not more than a year or two older than Maria, a handsome fellow with wavy hair and dark eyes. He loved to party and dance. That was how he met Maria, at a dance. He loved to drink and sometimes had to be taken home. Billy Watson loved the idea of a woman to be there for him. He was very affectionate and at times almost insatiable in the varied lovemaking he would pursue. As the months collected, Billy Watson continued to drink. He eventually lost his job with the county and would occasionally look for work, but his temper kept him from doing any permanent work.

Billy had heard about Maria's dream book a couple of years earlier and how she listed the dreams that she had. He was particularly interested in the dreams that talked about gold. No one ever got to see Maria's "Dream book."

Chapter 3

Jack had been working at his desk when the secretary called him and said that his mother was on the line. Jack Cummings' mother, Rita, very seldom communicated with her son. She had spent the last year and a half in Mesa Arizona, taking care of her father who was suffering from severe dementia. Jack had a premonition that this was not going to be a good call.

"Jack honey, it's finally happened." There was tension in Rita's voice and she could hardly get the words out. "It's your grandfather; he passed away early this morning. The EMT people said that he had a heart attack and just quietly quit breathing." Rita had been taking care of her father ever since he blacked out in his front yard almost two years earlier. Jack tried to figure out grandpa Ezra's age. He was born around the turn of the century, that would make him in his late nineties at the time of his death. Jack had heard stories about his grandfather and his great-grandfather. It seems both of those men had tales to tell of treasure hunting and Indians and gold.

Getting the time off was no problem as Jack had several weeks of vacation on the books. He took the first flight out of O'Hare airport to Phoenix Arizona. He had a window seat, but kept the shade pulled completely down. The afternoon sun shone directly into the window and the glare was known to give him headaches. He dozed most of the flight and the final approach to Phoenix Sky Harbor International airport roused him from his sleep. Jack was always one to travel light. His single suitcase contained his casual clothes, underwear, and of course his black suit.

He didn't check any baggage and was able to bypass the carousel. He went straight to the rental car counter, rented a midsized car and was out on Interstate-10 and heading East. It'd been years since Jack was in Phoenix. He had visited his grandfather as a teenager and that was the last time, he had seen him. He remembered Ezra Mitchell as a tall thin man with sparse white hair. Despite his gaunt frame, Ezra had a handshake that was like a vice. Jack couldn't tell if his grandfather was squeezing his hand on purpose or if it was just his way. Jack remembered that as a teen he would shake his grandfather's hand and squeezed back just as hard. The old man and the young boy with hands gripped tightly would stare into each other's eyes. There was a twinkle in the old man's eyes and Jack just never knew.

Jack raced the car down Interstate 10 and turned onto US route 60 toward Mesa. It was a cloudless summer sky and the temperatures climbed into the 90's before lunchtime. Air-conditioning was a necessity in this land. Jack remembered the few turns required and was soon pulling into the driveway of Ezra Mitchell's home. It was a large piece of land with a single-story home and a couple of outbuildings in the back of the lot. No one cultivated lawns in this part of the country but people were very unique and creative with the desert in their front yard.

Jack knocked on the front door and Rita opened it to greet him. The somberness of the occasion filled the air. Mother and son hugged each other. The occasion was a bit quiet and formal. Rita was over the initial sorrow and now concentrated on the tasks required to reverently put her father in his grave.

"Mom, is there anything that I can do or needs to be done?" Jack held his mother at arm's length. His mother always had her hair done, but now the gray was starting to show through.

"I've got everything under control but I'm sure there's something I'm missing. There will be a wake for the next two days, and Papa will be buried here."

Jack unpacked his bags in a spare bedroom and joined his mother in the kitchen. He let her do the talking as she needed to get a lot of issues off her chest. Rita wasn't sure if she wanted to live in the Phoenix area. Although she spent some time here taking care of her father, the desert and the harshness of the terrain were intimidating to most newcomers. Jack was the first to agree with her. The preciseness of his lifestyle and living in the Phoenix area were diametrical opposites. The couple of times he visited as a child, Jack noticed that his grandfather seemed to enjoy the challenge and the harshness of the land. The occasional scorpions and rattlesnakes were a mere nuisance to the people who lived here.

Jack asked if he could see the workshop of his grandfather that was in the back of the property. Rita got a ring with a few keys on it and told him to go explore.

There was a separate garage and an additional outbuilding on the backend of the property. Jack remembered that his grandfather was very good at making things, very good with his hands. The door to the workshop slid sideways on a metal rail. From the squeaking and grinding, the door let it be known that no one had opened the door in a long time. Cobwebs and dust covered about everything inside the door. He switched on the lights and as he looked about, a grin spread across his face. Every screwdriver had a hole, hammers were hung on peg boards in ascending sizes. Crescent wrenches were all in proper order. Hand tools each had a niche on the wall. Ezra's large power tools such as drill press, radial arm saw, table saw and overhead wench, all were covered with canvas. Jack took comfort in the neatness of this shop. Now he knew where his demand for preciseness originated.

The back part of the shop contained bins for various size pieces of wood. Ezra had it all graded according to kind and size. Jack wandered about, thinking of his grandfather. His hands slid over the various pieces of wood feeling the grain and wondering if there had been some purpose to them. Jack knew that his grandfather, Ezra, had been a veterinarian. That was an interesting thought. The same hands that sanded, cut, and nailed this wood would also be the hands that help heal animals and put the animals at ease while he performed some procedure.

Jack lingered in the back of the shop, the intense afternoon sunlight pouring in through dusty and weathered windowpanes. A noise from the front of the shop awakened him from his reveries. Rita was standing just inside the doorway, her arms folded across her chest. Her eyes took in all those things that entertained Jack and she too was amazed at the orderliness of everything.

"I don't think I've been in here for years, at least not since I started taking care of Ezra." Rita had no idea what some of the tools were. But she was fascinated with the neatness of everything. "I knew Papa was a stickler for orderliness, but this is a pleasant discovery." She wandered through the shop and ended up standing beside Jack looking at the different woods. "I've seen Papa's will, and he's leaving everything to me," Rita said, almost absently. "What am I to do with all of this? Can you use any of these tools?"

Jack looked at all the power tools and the well-kept hand tools. Most men desire tools and a workshop. The saying was certainly true, "The difference between men and boys are the price of the toys." He knew that none of this would go back with him to his apartment in Chicago. His eyes wandered over the darkened corners in the back of the wood shop, slowly coming to the realization that none of this would be his. Back in the corner stowed under a cache of wood were three old steamer trunks.

Chapter 4

Exploring would have to wait, there were more immediate tasks to be accomplished. Jack and Rita closed up the workshop and made ready for the wake that evening. Jack had some misgivings as he was new to the area and not familiar with any of his grandfather's friends. Jack was mildly aware of Ezra's standing in the community. He donned his black suit. He noticed a thin film of dust on his shoes. A quick wipe with a bath towel sufficed. Both he and Rita drove to the funeral home. It was still a bit early. He had some time to look about the different rooms of the home. Rita guessed that most of the people would be by after dinner. With nothing to do, Jack went outside and watched the sunset. The oranges and reds of the sky against the dark red mountains fashioned a sunset that was memorable. But this happened every night.

Guests started coming in and Jack stayed by his mother's side to welcome them. Men in suits on their way home from work dropped in. Farmers and laborers in overalls made a point of coming by. All of them wished Jack and Rita their heartfelt sympathies. Jack noticed that a lot of the people at the funeral home had the darkened skin and high cheekbones common of the Indian peoples.

Jack asked Rita why there were so many Indians in attendance. Rita said that Ezra had done a lot of pro-bono work on the Indian reservation over the years. She guessed that the Indians were paying last respects. Jack noticed a young woman among the throng of Indian people. Her coal black hair was tied in a large braid coming down her back. Their eyes met from across the room. Jack was a bit uncomfortable as she caught him looking at her. His only defense was a slight nod of his head in her direction. Maria pushed her way through the people to Jack.

"Ezra Mitchell was well-liked in this community. Thank you for coming," Jack stammered with his hands in his pockets.

"I'm Maria Two-Crows. Dr. Mitchell was my mentor. Yes, he was well-liked by almost everyone and…."

"I just got into town…" Jack got interrupted.

"Oh, you must be the grandson. My grandfather told me you would be here."

"I don't think I told anyone I was coming," Jack said somewhat defensively.

Maria smiled, "My grandfather is very old and he is a shaman. He told me that a tall man who would have long skinny legs like that of a road runner would come. He said that you would run a lot, but not go anywhere."

Jack didn't know what to say. He mentioned that Ezra Mitchell was his grandfather but they hadn't been close.

Maria told Jack that she knew Dr. Mitchell since she was a young girl. He would come to the reservation a couple of times a week to help heal any of the livestock there. She remembered that she had been a bit of a pest when he first visited the reservation. The doctor made her his assistant when he had to treat any of the animals. Over the years, Maria gained a wealth of knowledge on veterinary medicine. When Dr. Mitchell became too ill, Maria stepped in and did the things that needed to be done. She visited the doctor many times while his daughter, Rita did the housekeeping. Maria would borrow some of the doctor's instruments, but she needed him to write prescriptions.

Jack listened with rapt attention to Maria's story. He never had any idea that his grandfather was interested in the Apache culture. Maria told Jack that her grandfather, who was a shaman and practiced his medicines, got along well with Ezra Mitchell. The two men would talk long into the night.

Rita noticed from across the room that Jack was talking to an Apache girl. She wandered over to Jack and Maria and extended her hand to Maria. "Thank you for coming, my father thought very highly of you." Her nonchalance gave Jack a hint that she knew Maria. Maria accepted her handshake and drew Rita close and hugged her.

"I see you've met my son, Jack. He's come from Chicago to help me through this ordeal. Maria. You must come by the house after all this is finished. I'd like to give you the rest of father's veterinary tools and perhaps we can talk about some of the stuff that's in his workshop outback."

Rita took one of Maria's hands and patted it with her own. This was somewhat a subliminal signal to Maria that everything was well in hand. Rita excused herself saying that she needed to talk to some other people who had come in the door.

Jack and Maria talked for some time. Jack was unusually curious about the culture and customs of the Apache Indian, and Maria was only too happy to accommodate his questioning. Maria reached back into the history and told him of the Apache life on the plains. She told of the westward movement of the Apache Indian nation. The encroachment of the Comanche tribes forced the Apache to seek lands farther and farther West. The plains buffalo fed several different Indian tribes. Before the introduction of horses, the Apache would run on foot amid the lumbering herds of buffalo. It was this necessity that forced the Apache men to become athletic. It was rumored that an Apache man could cover 50 miles a day amid the heat of the western sun. Jack was somewhat in awe of the history that Maria related.

At the end of the evening, Jack and Rita headed back to Ezra's home. Jack had plenty of things to ponder about his grandfather. The ride home was in silence. Jack drove, but his mind wandered. He never thought his grandfather would have any ties to the local minorities. Ezra's career as a veterinarian was well documented and rather commonplace. But, his workshop and his extensive pro bono work on the Apache reservation were new attributes. Mix in the severity of the landscape for hundreds of miles in each direction. Jack was at a loss to make these pieces of his grandfather's life fit a rationale that he could understand.

Ezra Mitchell was buried and everyone headed back to their home. Jack took Rita to the lawyer's office and the will was read. It was as Rita had said. All of Dr. Mitchell's earthly possessions now belonged to his daughter. Everything seems straightforward, but Rita wondered, if her father had that much interest in the Native American cultures why he hadn't donated any of his possessions or bequeathed any monies to them.

Rita had to make some decisions. She now had two households, and she was in a quandary as to which one to keep. She had a home in Ohio that she had closed when she had to take care of her father. In the little more than a year that she had been in the Phoenix area taking care of her father, Rita had become familiar with the heat of the southwest. Perhaps Jack could help her make a decision.

Chapter 5

Maria came by Ezra's house as promised. Jack, Rita, and Maria sat at the kitchen table with coffee and a plate of bagels. Rita mentioned again the close relationship that her father had with young Maria. There was a room at the back of the house that Dr. Mitchell used as an examination room for animals. This was in addition to the facilities at the clinic where he had worked. The shelves and drawers in the examining room had various stainless-steel devices and lots of medicines. The three of them wandered into the small clinic. The center of the room was dominated by a large steel examination table. Maria said she would be ever so grateful if she could get the examination table out to the reservation. Jack quietly smiled because this table would not go through the door in one piece. Maria said her boyfriend had a pickup that she could use to transport all of this. And so, they three spent hours cleaning out the room and boxing the small devices. Maria promised to return the next day if Jack would help her load the pickup.

Rita brought out some of her father's everyday work clothes. Ezra's tall skinny frame matched that of his grandson. Jack tried on the jeans and even the dusty and scarred up old cowboy boots. He didn't say anything, but even though the clothes fit, there was an uneasy feeling. Wrinkled clothes and scarred boots were not anywhere to be found in Jack Cummings' closets. But for the tasks that had to be done around the house, they filled the need.

The next morning, Maria showed up at the back of Ezra's house in an old Chevy pickup. Dents and faded red oxide paint were the most distinguishing characteristics. Jack was able to get the examination table disassembled, out the back door and loaded onto the truck. Maria loaded cardboard boxes with various stainless-steel instruments. There were jars of various medicinal liquids, tubes of pastes, and rolls of assorted bandages.

Maria turned the key and the old truck sprang to life. There is a bit of vibration but everything seemed to work well. Jack slid into the passenger side and closed the door. He looked for a seatbelt, there wasn't any. Maria shifted to reverse and the truck slid out of the driveway. The gearshift occupied the center of the cab. She double clutched and smoothly moved through the gears. Both windows were down and the sun was merciless. As they slid along the interstate, Maria announced that this would be about a two-hour trip to San Carlos on the Apache reservation. Jack and Maria made small talk for the most of the trip. Maria mentioned that she worked in a small restaurant in Apache Junction. When Maria asked what he did for a living, Jack just said that he was an accountant. The last half hour of the trip was on a back road that had been paved about 50 years ago. The springs in the truck got a real workout.

Jack watched the scenery slip by and it never changed. The outcroppings of rock towered 100 to 200 feet above them on both sides and the gullies were filled with cactus, low growing tumbleweed and mesquite. The layers of rock only varied the colors of red or magenta. The sun as usual, persecuted the countryside with over 100° temperatures. Clouds didn't have a chance to exist in these temperatures. It was the red earth against the blue sky.

As they pulled into San Carlos, occasional huts dotted either side of the road. all of them were small one-story homes made out of dried cement stuck onto chicken wire. Some of the homes had a whitewash on the walls. Windows and doors were left open to capture any hint of breeze. An occasional chicken would be scratching in the dirt and weeds of the front yard. Several homes had disabled relics of automobiles. There is nothing in the Arizona air to promote rusting, the vehicles were going to be there a long while.

As Maria drove the truck slowly through the dusty streets, Jack was making some mental notes about the affluence of the town in general. San Carlos, Arizona, was generally considered as the poorest community in the United States. The per capita income stood somewhere around $11,000 per year. The land was generally terrible for agriculture, not enough people live there to qualify for any sort of government assistance, other than what came through the Bureau of Indian Affairs. Jack saw firsthand what the American government did to the Apache culture. Jack decided to find some facts and figures concerning this condition.

They pulled up to a salt box style house that had been abandoned. Large weeds guarded the walkway and the door was slightly ajar. Maria led the way in and they stood on the concrete floor with trash and pieces of wood as the only evidence of any occupancy. The kitchen showed a small sink but that was the only thing to convince you that it was a kitchen. Jack tried to spigot and all he got were belches of air and brown water.

Jack brought in some wrenches, and with several pieces of the table he proceeded to set up the steel examining table in the kitchen area. Cupboard space and water were the two ingredients for the decision. As Jack was assembling the table, several people in the neighborhood came by to watch him work. As the steel monstrosity began to take shape, people recognized its use and they all nodded their head in affirmation. Loitering down the street, a few young men were discussing this intrusion into their life. It was bad enough that a woman was the center of attention, but she had the help of a white man. Apache reservation land was not generally open for the white race.

Sundown was quickly approaching as Jack and Maria Two Crows completed the assembly of the table and cleaning of the kitchen.

"Jack, how about some supper and you can stay overnight?" Jack just shrugged his shoulders. He was easy to please. "You can meet my grandfather. He and your grandfather were close friends."

"Maybe tomorrow morning you and I could go for a run to the lake?" Jack wasn't sure. He thought he saw a slight smile on Maria's face. Maria closed the windows and both the front and side door to the house. She had new locks that she placed on the doors. Jack was leaning against the truck as she completed. "No sense tempting honest folk," as she climbed into the truck.

Maria drove the truck a short distance and pulled up to another small building similar to the one they were just at. An old man stood in the doorway. The light behind him made him a dark outline. Maria ran up to him, threw her arms around him and kissed him on his forehead.

"Sichoo, it is always good to see you. I brought a friend this evening. His name is Jack Cummings. He is Dr. Ezra Cummings grandson. You remember Dr. Cummings, you and he used to sit and talk into the late night.

Jack strode up the path and in the light from the house he made out to features of Charlie "Red Fox" Morgan. The old man was bent over and came up to Jack shoulder. He had not lost any hair, but all of it was snow white. His face was his wrinkled as a well-weathered apple. His eyes clouded by cataracts. Jack shook his hand and felt the grip that was uncommonly firm on such an aged man.

Maria pushed past both of the men, went into the small house and somewhere turned on an electric light. She moved into the kitchen area and started mixing some things together. Jack followed Charlie Red Fox into the living area of the house. Some shelves along one wall were strewn with small bottles of various things. There was nothing that Jack would easily identify. An old TV set sat across from two wooden chairs, a set of rabbit ears on top small balls of aluminum foil cringed onto the ends. One corner held a wooden table that was strewn with scattered papers, a black feather and a well-used coffee mug.

Charlie motioned with one hand for Jack to take a chair. He backed to the other chair using both hands to hold on to the arms and eased himself in. "Been in Arizona long?" was Charlie's first attempt to break the ice.

"Just a couple of days to help my mother bury my grandfather. I must admit that the heat here is unrelenting." Charlie nodded in ascent as he kept slowly rubbing his hands together.

"There have been worse years. It's the water that's important." Charlie rambled on about conserving water. Jack just let him do the talking. Many people said Jack was a good conservationist. He just knew to keep his mouth shut most of the time.

After about a half an hour Maria motioned for the two men to come into the kitchen. Sundown had long passed. At the table were three plates, spoons, and small plastic bottles of water. Maria had made some large tortillas and there was a bowl of black beans and chunks of onion. Jack sat between Maria and her grandfather and watched to see what they did. Tortillas in one hand, and spoon the other. Black beans scooped from the bowl, and rolled up in the tortilla. two per person and a bottle of warm water. that was dinner. Maria apologized for the bottled water. She said that the Bureau of Indian Affairs had been contacted to repair water line. It has been two months and no one has yet appeared.

One side of the front room had a wooden bed frame. The mattress was a rope twined back and forth across the sides and covered by a couple of blankets. An identical frame on the other side of the room was Charlie's bed. Maria curled up on the floor. She wished Charlie and Jack a good night and turned out the light. Jack noticed with the lights out it was seriously dark in this house.

The house faced East to meet the rising sun. Two grimy windows were the only filters of the intense sunlight. Jack swung his legs out over the frame and his back muscles protested this kind of bed. Jack saw that Maria was already up and washing her face and arms in the kitchen sink. Everyone slept with their clothes on. As Jack wandered into the kitchen, Maria turned and put a finger to her lips to caution Jack from making noise.

Maria whispered to him, "Do you want to go for a run before it gets too hot?"

"How far do you have in mind, I don't have my running shoes?"

"It's only a couple of miles. We'll just jog down to the lake and back." Maria seemed a bit anxious to get Jack to run with her. Jack had some soft soled shoes and didn't think that would be much of an impediment to the jogging. Maria took the lead and jogged down the gravel road that they had come in the day before. Jack kept up with her, four or five paces behind. After about a mile or so, Maria put about 50 to 75 yards between Jack and herself. There is no talking and the only noise is that of the feet hitting the hard ground. Whatever bit of sweat he worked up evaporated quickly in the morning air.

Jack felt a bit uneasy about the girl having such a large lead on him. He picked up the pace considerably and was beginning to close that gap. He was rounding a bend in the road when he saw, ambling along the opposite side of the road a very large, black and white beaded gila monster. It wasn't moving very fast, and its waddling gait was easy to avoid. Jack had heard somewhere that these did not make very good pets. In fact, he had heard that this animal had a poisonous bite. The brief encounter turned out to be more of an incentive for Jack to catch up to Maria. It took a little bit over 40 minutes for them to reach San Carlos reservoir. Maria's two- or 3-mile jaunt turned out to be almost 5 miles.

For Jack this was an excellent workout. He had worked up a healthy sweat and was breathing deeply. Maria came up to him and offered a liter bottle of water that she had been carrying. Jack looked at her and noticed the woman had barely broken a sweat. Jack remembered a line from an old Clint Eastwood movie, "A man has got to know his limitations." It never said anything about a woman.

Jack told Maria that he had seen a lizard that he thought perhaps might be a gila monster. "Were these lizards to be avoided?" Maria looked a bit concerned and told Jack that there had not been a citing of gila lizard on reservation land for some time, but yes, avoid them as they have a poisonous bite.

The two stood at the edge of San Carlos reservoir. It was obvious that the level of the reservoir had receded a couple of feet. The water looked a bit murky, and the sun coming up from the East gave a harsh glint across the surface of the lake. Jack picked up a flat stone and skipped it out across the surface. A couple of more draws on the bottle of water and Jack was ready to return.

"Jack, no need to take it easy on me because I'm a girl. Let's get back before grandfather becomes awake."

Jack thought to himself as he started the return trip, "Yeah, right! I'll be lucky if I can keep within 20 feet of your rear end."

About halfway back to the settlement, a small cloud of dust could be seen. As they continued, the dust cloud became an old beat up pickup. Both Jack and Maria watched the truck approach as they continued their run. As a truck passed Maria, it swerved hard to the right, kicking up more dust and the pebbles. It definitely had Jack in the crosshairs to run him down. As Jack jumped aside, he saw two young Indian men in the cab. The truck sped down the gravel road. Jack turned and watched through the churned-up dust cloud. Hands on his hips, he watched and wondered, "What the hell was that all about?" Jack and Maria watched the truck disappear into the dust cloud.

"OK. What the hell was that?" Jack threw it out to Maria for an explanation. "You have any idea why they would do that?"

"I saw them and a couple of other fellows last night standing a few houses away, watching as you and I dragged things into the abandoned house. Jack, your guess is good as mine. Thank goodness you were quick enough to avoid the truck."

Jack and Maria completed the run and quietly entered Charlie Morgan's home. Charlie was in the kitchen making breakfast. He had a pan of water on the stove that was about to boil. He sprinkled about a half a handful of coffee grounds into the pan. Last night's pot of beans was back on the other burner. He added two scrambled eggs and added some onion to the bean pot. As Jack sat at the table, a slight grin appeared. He remembered the old adage, "Breakfast is the most important meal of the day."

The breakfast ritual was the same as dinner. Each took a large tortilla and spoon whatever was in the pot on to the tortilla and rolled it up. Maria mentioned to her grandfather that they had seen a gila monster along the route. She reminded both men that it been a couple of years since anyone had seen one of those on the reservation. Jack asked her to tell about the two Indian boys and a pickup who attempted to run him over. Did all visitors to the reservation get this special attention? Charlie thought about this for a moment.

"Jack Cummings, you plan on coming back to the reservation?" Charlie leaned forward, elbows on the table awaiting an answer.

"I suppose so. There are a number of other things that Maria would like to bring out to the reservation."

Charlie thought it wise to give some advice. "Have Maria bring you when you decide to come."

Maria started the engine to the old pickup and Jack knew it was time to leave. Jack shook hands with Charlie Morgan and thanked him for his hospitality. He expressed his desire to return to the reservation and to talk further. Charlie made a motion with his hand that meant safe voyage. Jack closed the door, leaned out the window and raised his right hand to acknowledge the old man. The truck wandered down the gravel road that Jack had encountered the lizard. In a little while, they turned onto a paved highway that led back to town. It was a two-hour trip and most of the time was spent in silence. Jack paid little attention to the meaning of the lizard and the errant pickup truck. Maria on the other hand had picked up on her grandfather's warning.

Jack idly watched Maria as she navigated the dirt road and finally onto the highway. She handled the gearshift with ease, even 'double-clutching' when needed. He noticed that although her bronze skin quite similar to the rest of the Apache culture, her facial features were a bit less in keeping. Where most of the Apache people had round faces, Maria's bone structure gave her a longer, thinner look. He had already seen her lithe and toned body give him a workout that he barely completed. He was sure that she must have several men calling.

She pulled up in front of Ezra Mitchell's home and thanked Jack for all his help and asked him to convey her thanks to Rita for all the medical equipment. She told Jack that she had to work for a few days and would find out if there were any Apache men who could make use of the hand tools.

Chapter 6

Maria pulled away from the house and smoothly moved the pick-up through the gears. The trip took are about 20 minutes to pull into the parking lot behind an apartment building. She had a small walk-up apartment on the fourth floor. Opening the door to the apartment, she immediately could smell tobacco smoke and perhaps beer. Billy Watson had been sitting in front of the TV for some time: ashtray full of butts, and several collapsed beer cans littering a plywood coffee table. Billy was snoring through a daytime soap opera. No sense waking him. Maria had realized early in her life there were certain characteristics that differentiated the red man from the white. One most notable was the Indian's inability to metabolize alcohol. It seems there is an enzyme that the American Indian does not possess. Women also have a deficiency of this enzyme.

She took a quick shower, fixed her hair in a long braid, and donned a hideous brown uniform of a blouse and skirt. As she was leaving, she put the truck keys beside Billy's pack of cigarettes. He was sure to see that when he awoke. The old 15 speed bicycle stood in the hallway. The paint job was hardly recognizable, but there were two shiny chrome rearview mirrors attached to the handlebars. Out the door and down the stairs with the bicycle balanced on her shoulder. Maria often wondered if it was possible to ride the bicycle down the flights of steps. The restaurant wasn't far away. The food was passable. This independent restaurant was somewhere in the group of IHOP/Denny's kind of menu.

Billy heard the door shut, but he still kept his eyes closed for a few minutes long. He knew that she would not be back for several hours and this gave him the opportunity to continue his search of their small apartment. The only reason that Billy lived with Maria was to find her book.

Billy heard that Maria had kept a small diary and in it, she would recount some of the dreams that she had. When Maria was an adolescent, she started having strange dreams. She dreamt that she was a crow flying over the Apache reservation. In her dream, she would look down and see different rock formations. She found the dreams to be unsettling. She asked her grandfather what the dreams meant. He asked her several questions and sat for some time rubbing his hands together. He finally suggested to her that she should write down the dreams and perhaps the meaning would become clear to her. The dreams didn't happen often, but over the years she filled up a small diary with her recollections. She mentioned this to some of her classmates. Some thought that she had the gift of visions; others thought that she was a bit mentally unbalanced, but everyone wanted to read her "Dream book." In a couple of her descriptions of the dream she mentioned seeing some of the Apache gold. The novelty of reading her dream book wore off when no more mention of the gold or the location appeared. Maria had a hiding spot in one of the posts of the old bed in her grandfather's house. Some of the brash comments that the other kids made put Maria on edge. She confessed to her grandfather one time that she wished that she had not mentioned any of her dreams. Billy patiently scoured the bedroom of the apartment for the hidden book. He was sure this dream look was a key to the hidden Peralta gold. He continued his search, looking for loose floor boards of the apartment, no luck.

He was low on cigarettes and out of beer. This meant to trip to a neighborhood bar called "The Road Runner." It was late in the day when he walked through the door. The subdued lighting and cool air made this an enticing watering hole. Dust covered most of the decorations and all of the bottles that were rarely used. Billy threw a leg over a barstool and sat next to a drinking buddy.

"Did you find the book?" Otis was one to come straight to the point. Otis was several drinks ahead of Billy, and his face showed it. His eyes were red rimmed and watery. His wrinkled clothes had absorbed several days sweat.

Billy pursed his lips and slowly shook his head as a negative. He thumped to fist lightly onto the bar. "Dammit, Otis, I've scoured that whole apartment and the book is not there. I'm trying to figure where else she could use as a hiding place. She was living at her grandfather's place while in high school. I guess I gotta go out to the reservation and spend some time with Charlie Red Fox. But I got to go when Maria is not around. Otis, I need a reason to visit the old man."

Otis was not the man to solve such dilemmas. He furrowed his brow as if deep in thought. Billy thought it was a rhetorical question, but Otis was drunk and Otis was serious. "Hey Billy, why don't you just ask the old man for a charm, or a spell to help you find something that is lost." Billy took a long swig of beer and looked at Otis with wide eyes.

"Dammit Otis, that is got to be the most brilliant thing that you have said in a long time! If I can get the old man to go out looking for some herbs, I'll be able to give the house a once over. Yeah! That's what I'll do. I just got a find out what shift Maria is working." Billy took a long swig out of the beer bottle and sat there in quiet. He took a second-long swig and had the look on his face as if he had just solved Einstein's unified field theory.

Jack and Rita were busy at Ezra's house. They gathered together several periodicals, technical papers, and a couple of notebooks that Ezra used to keep track of his patients. Rita placed all of the material into a large black plastic garbage bag. She secured it with a tie and left that and two other bags on the kitchen table.

"Jack when do you plan to take these to the reservation?" Jack rubbed his hand over his forehead, closed his eyes and thought a moment.

"I guess I'll take all this stuff and put it in the back seat. There are some hand tools that I can put in the trunk and Maria can escort me when she has a day off." Jack was beginning to look forward to Maria's company. Jack called and left a message on Maria's answering machine. He told of the materials that he had accumulated and was anxious to see Maria again and take this to the reservation. He mentioned that if she was not occupied to come by the house tomorrow and they could take his car to the reservation.

Maria got the message, but she had to work the next afternoon. The next morning, she donned the hideous brown uniform and took the 10 speed over to the Mitchell house. Billy Watson lying in bed quietly observed Maria in the uniform. "She's gone to work dayshift!" Billy's mind was working in overdrive. This would be a good time to have a look at her grandfather's house on the reservation. Quickly, he slid on his jeans, scuffed boots, and an old shirt. He grabbed his hat on the way out and headed the truck for the reservation.

Maria made it over to the Ezra Mitchell home and she could see Jack and his mother moving about the kitchen. She knocked on the kitchen door and Maria motioned her to come in. Breakfast was some bagels and black coffee. Jack showed her the periodicals and the documents that he thought should go into her veterinary clinic. He had a few hand tools that he put into the trunk. Jack noticed that the scuffed boots had a thin film of dust on them. Jack took a couple of napkins and wiped the boots. They set off for the reservation, Maria drove.

The trip to the reservation was a bit shorter; Jack's rented car definitely was faster than that old pickup. When they hit the dirt road, Maria slowed the car to a walk to keep the dust plumes down. She was about to turn the corner to her grandfather's house when she saw Billy Watson's pickup parked in front. She stopped completely and tried to understand why Billy Watson would be visiting Charlie Red Fox Morgan. She sat there about 15 to 20 minutes, just watching. Finally, Billy Watson came out of the adobe with Charlie red Fox. Billy shook his hand and gave him a hug. The beat up old pickup cough to life and was gone. Maria pulled the car in front of her grandfather's house; there were some questions that needed answering.

Charlie was still standing in front of the house when Maria and Jack pulled up. Jack said that he would take the documents over to the soon to be veterinary clinic. Maria walked her grandfather inside and sat down.

"Sichoo, why was Billy Watson here this morning?" Maria was always very direct. Charlie sat for a few moments rubbing his hands together.

"The young boy came to me and asked for help. He asked me if I had any charms or medicine bag that would help him to get a job."

"That's all? He didn't ask you for anything more?" Maria couldn't figure out was why he came that early in the morning.

"I made him a medicine bag and he sat here while I put it together. I had to go hunt for a couple of things. But he stayed in the house and waited while I went out."

Jack returned to the house and knocked on the open door before entering. "Mr. Morgan, I have some tools from my grandfather's workshop that I would like to donate to any of your people who can make use of it. If you like, I can put them here by this bed."

The small clutter of hand tools that made a pile at the end of Maria's bed were indistinguishable from the rest of the clutter and dust of Charlie Red Fox's home. "I have some power tools that I'd like to bring but I wasn't sure if you had the required electricity. Guess I'll have to make a second trip." A slight smile was on Jack's face, he was quite pleased with himself.

Charlie was sitting in a chair and motioned Jack to come over to him. He grabbed Jack's shirt a bit and hinted that Jack should bend over. Charlie's wrinkled fingers picked up a small sack on a piece of rawhide. He reached up and put it over Jack's head and let it hang down. He pointed the finger to Jack and told him to always wear this while he was on the reservation. "There are some spirits that live in these mountains that require visitors to have protection."

Chapter 7

Jack spent some time wandering through Ezra's workshop again. Rita was already in there with a fox-tail brush and dusting rags. As Jack wandered through, he came to the realization that most of the pieces of carpentry equipment were so large that they would have to be transported separately. Jack laid out a lot of the hand tools could be put in some boxes. Maria came in and wondered at the sight of all the orderliness. He asked Maria if there was anyone on the reservation who could make use of these tools. That's when he thought of the trunks in the back of the shop almost hidden under stores of spare wood.

Jack pulled a small steamer trunk hidden underneath a rack of different sized wood pieces. He was amazed that despite the small size of the trunk, it was incredibly heavy. Years of sawdust had built up on the top. The metal latch had initials stamped on it, "L M." were still distinguishable through the scratches and gouges in the metal hasp. Jack and his mother surrounded the trunk for a grand opening. Loosening a catch and throwing the lid back, sunlight streamed in for the first time in over 50 years. Jack reached in and pulled out a small pick, a shovel with half a handle, a 2-foot-long pike, a large cold chisel and a couple of short handled sledgehammers.

As the tools lay on the floor, Rita gasped slightly and brought her hands up to her mouth. Jack gave her a quizzical look. It took Rita a few moments to let this discovery sink in. She stooped and rubbed the handles of a couple of the implements.

"I didn't think there was any truth to that story," Rita said. It took a minute or two for the evidence from the trunk to sink in. "Jack, there is another chapter of the Mitchell family. This story concerns your great-grandfather, Luther Mitchell." Rita searched through her memories where to start.

"It seems that your great-grandfather Luther was a veterinarian. He was living in Texas and was contacted in the early 1900's by the Department of Agriculture to inspect cattle purchased by the United States government from Mexico. Dr. Mitchell routinely crossed into Mexico to inspect herds of cattle. It was on one such trip that he met a young officer in the Mexican army who was in the army stockade. During conversations with the young officer, Dr. Mitchell found out that the officer had been jailed for some thefts. The young officer asked Dr. Mitchell to take his family into the United States and see to their welfare. The only thing that the officer had to trade of value was a map that had been in his family for a couple of generations. The officer said that this map would lead one to the mines that the Peralta's had worked some 80 years before. Luther agreed to take the soldier's family to the United States. In a long round case, the soldier gave Dr. Mitchell, was a rolled-up piece of rawhide leather. On one side was a map with strange symbols burned into the hide.

Luther tried to decipher the markings on the map, but he came to the conclusion that the markings would be very difficult to interpret without being physically present on the land. He made a mental note that someday, he would have to visit Phoenix Arizona and the Apache reservation. The case lay forgotten in the back corner of a bedroom closet.

Luther continued with his veterinary profession and eventually married a woman, Caroline Donnelly, from Oklahoma. They had a small family of two girls, Anna and Eunice, and one boy, Ezra. As Ezra grew, Luther would often take the boy with him to the various ranches in the county. Luther encouraged the boy to lay hands on the afflicted animal and Luther would cover the boy's hands with his own and guide the small fingers to touch and feel the problem.

Ezra was quick-witted and understood what his father was showing him. But what he liked best was the contact between him, his father, and the animal. There was always a smell of the animal, the barn, and his father's sweat that made each of these encounters indelible on the boy. As Ezra grew into a teenager, he felt that with his father's hands on his, they could cure any animal of any disease and repair any broken bone.

The logical conclusion was for Ezra to attend college and earn a degree in veterinary science. Ezra graduated with a degree in veterinary science and followed in his father's footsteps. They both shared the same practice. As

Luther grew older, he let his son take over the majority of the work. One day quite by accident, while looking for some shoes in his closet, Luther spied a black cylindrical container leaning in the corner, hiding behind a closet full of clothes. He pulled out the tube and stretched the roll a piece of rawhide on the kitchen table. Cryptic markings filled the hide. Luther's fingers traced over each of the markings as he remembered that officer in Mexico. The stories of the Peralta gold were legend. Hundreds of pounds of gold lay hidden somewhere in the Arizona desert. There was a litany of names of people who went into the desert looking for the riches. Many never came back and none ever caught a scent of that immense wealth. But Luther had a map! It didn't take long for fantasies to light up his eyes. His son was in charge of the clinic. What was holding this 70-year-old man from seeking his fame and fortune? He had the map! He and Ezra would talk things over but one thing Luther was sure of. He was headed to Phoenix. Ezra would have nothing to do with his father's fantasy. Man into his 70s, searching the deserts of Arizona for treasure, where others before him had disappeared, is not something he could agree.

Luther packed his bags, stowed them with a trunk full of old tools and the precious map in the trunk of his beat-up Studebaker. He left a note for Ezra explaining where he was headed. Phoenix was a good three' days drive from Lubbock Texas, about 700 miles. Luther had done some research on the Peralta gold. Mixed in with the Peralta gold story was the tale of the lost Dutchman mine. But Luther had the map!

Coming off of US route 60, Luther pulled into the first motel in the small village of Apache Junction. The dust, the heat, and glare of evening sun made him exhausted. He found a small hotel and immediately bathed all of the exhaustion down the drain. The lights of a local diner shone in the twilight. All of the problems and questions could wait till tomorrow but a hearty steak was uppermost in his mind. The next couple days Luther spent wandering about the town asking innocuous questions about Peralta gold. He learned about Jim Haley's ranch." Rita paused.

She smoothed her skirt and continued, "I was a little girl when this took place. I remember my father telling me that Luther went to the Haley ranch. The people at the ranch advised him not to go into the Superstition Mountains during this time of the year. He went into the mountains despite everyone's advice. He was there two days and died under mysterious circumstances. If you want to know more, I would suggest talking to the people at the ranch."

Jack looked into the bottom of the chest and saw that it was lined with an old dried out oilcloth. The oilcloth had a large wrinkle running the length of the box as if covering something. Jack reached in and gingerly pulled back the oilcloth. Underneath there was a rolled-up piece of cowhide tied with an unusual looking rawhide strap. Gingerly pulling the rolled-up cowhide, and unrolling it, Jack and the two women anxiously waited, as it was spread out over trunk. The markings that were burned into the hide, indicated that it is some sort of map. Maria looked at it and gave a small laugh.

"I've seen this before." Maria's hands were lightly touching the different markings. "I am almost sure that this map was the one that the lady who helped Herman Weiss was selling for a small price. There is a copy in our Indian Museum. We can take this and compare it." Jack and Rita lost their enthusiasm. This map was all over Southwest, and no one's found the gold.

Jack was spellbound by the tale that his mother told. These old men, his great-grandfather and grandfather, had led some interesting lives. Only the best equipped and hearty white man ventured into the Superstition Mountains during this time of the year. Her grandfather had told her many stories about the gods who resided in these mountains. It seems that if the explorer did not have Apache blood, misfortune or illness would befall them.

Chapter 8

There was a ranch a few miles out of town situated at the foot of the Superstition Mountains. Jim Haley's spread the J-bar-H ranch, entertained treasure hunters, rock hounds, and ill-equipped nimrods looking for the lost Dutchman mine. Jack pulled up to the front of the main house. He could see several cars parked out front; he hoped he wasn't intruding. The door opened and Jack identified himself. He asked to speak to Jim Haley. Man, with gray sideburns and gray mustache said that Jim Haley had passed away a few years ago.

"I'm George Haley, his son. What can I do for you?"

"I'm Jack Cummings, the great-grandson of Luther Mitchell. Luther had a son named Ezra, my grand-father, who died recently. I've been helping to clean up grandpa Ezra's personal effects. One of the things I've come across were some papers concerning Luther Mitchell. I was told that Luther Mitchell visited your ranch shortly before his death. If anyone here has any information on my great-grandfather's last days, I would be forever grateful."

George invited young Jack into a front sitting room and told him, "I was a young kid when Mr. Mitchell came to the ranch. He talked of having this map that he said would lead him to the Peralta mines. My father, Jim Haley, invited Luther in for something cold to drink and rest. My dad's hospitality was well-known to ranchers, cowboys and prospectors. Luther was greeted by several of these people. He asked the people who were there if they had any insights to the lost Dutchman mine or the Peralta gold. I remember a couple of older fellows had offered anecdotes about people who went into the desert. One universal thread tied all of these stories together. Not many returned from the superstition mountains. Remains were found months later, but coyotes and pumas devoured most of the remains. Thank goodness for dental records."

Luther mentioned his map and how he had procured it. He was confident he would not be wandering aimlessly. He just needed a guide and a couple of pack animals to accompany him on this quest. It was almost unanimous that Mr. Mitchell should not go into the mountains. It was well before noon time and the temperatures were now climbing close to the hundreds. By this afternoon the desert heat would be unbearable. He knew that there was some validity in what the other men said, but he was so close. He had the map!

After much conversation among the people there, no one was able to dissuade the old man. Dad took Luther aside and told him that if Luther could wait some time, Jim would be willing to guide him into the foothills of the Superstition Mountains. Jim added that he had several business dealings in Phoenix that would keep him gone from the ranch for about 3 to 5 days. Luther nodded that that was acceptable to him and he would be willing to pay for his stay at the ranch and any expenses for the short expedition.

Bright and early the next morning, Jim Haley's truck drove off in the direction of Phoenix. Luther wandered about the main buildings of the ranch. he did a cursory examination of a couple of the horses and heads of cattle that were in the corral. The bar-h ranch took very good care of their animals. A couple of the cowboys took a pause in their chores to chat with Luther. They said that they had listened to his story the night before and were interested in helping him. If Luther had the map, the cowboys could take him to the foothills of the Superstition Mountains. Luther thought a moment and asked, "How long will it take you to saddle the horses and pack the mule?"

It was late morning when the three of them trotted northward. Luther hadn't been on a horse for some time and now was rudely reminded of what several hours bumping along in the saddle would do to a 70+ physique. The vegetation on the dark red soil was scattered. Occasional saguaro cactus and barrel cactus with palo verde trees would be landmarks. Different varieties of sagebrush filled in between the cactus. Every now and then Luther would take out a piece of paper, study it and then scan the surroundings. Every mile or so, he would change direction but generally he was headed north into the Superstition Mountains. By late afternoon, Luther Mitchell was leaning over in the saddle, his bent frame absorbing all of the vibrations of horseback travel. The cowboys noticed this and picked a campsite for the night. The three of them quickly set the tent, built a hearth, unsaddled Luther's horse and unloaded the pack mule. Luther began to feel better having gotten off the horse. He told the cowboys that he was in fine shape, had plenty of food, and even had a small pistol for protection. They could go back to the ranch and come back and pick him up in two days. The cowboys looked at each other and looked back at the old man. He seemed in fine spirits and had plenty of water. They mounted up and took off at a gallop hoping to make it back by sunrise. That wasn't going to happen. They camped about 15 miles from Luther and made it back to the ranch early the next morning.

It was two days later that Jim Haley made it back from Phoenix. He was about a half a day early. He looked about and couldn't find the old man. He started asking where Luther Mitchell was. The cowboys told him they had taken him out two days earlier and were about to go retrieve him. Jim Haley was furious! He reminded the cowboys of how severe the environment and the weather can be here. The man was 70+ years old and not accustomed to the Arizona heat. His last words to them were, "Saddle up and bring extra water!"

They rode hard most of the day, stopping only to rest the horses. It was about sundown when they arrived to the camp where they left Luther Mitchell. From a distance it was visible that the campsite had been pillaged. They were careful not to bring the horses into the campsite or to walk over any potential clues. The tent had collapsed and several articles were strewn about the campsite. The horse and mule were gone. Each man took a section of the ground and scanned it for any possible information. While there were scrape marks on the ground there was nothing to identify whether a man's boot or animals paw print was involved. One of the cowboys found the old man's revolver laying a couple of paces from the hearth and gave it to Jim Haley. As he handed it to Jim he said, "It looks like it's been fired three times."

Jim looked at the revolver. Covered with dust but upon an inspection three shells were spent. As he looked it over, he saw that it was a small .38 caliber weapon. Something you might see in the holster of a police officer. It was okay for defense against small game but if against a mountain lion, maybe the noise would scare the animal off. Jim asked one of the cowboys to find a long strip of white cloth and to tie it far up on one of the close by cactus. This would help when a search party came, they would make it straight to the camp and it would provide a point of reference for people searching the area close by.

Several search parties were organized and combed the surrounding area but to no avail. Weeks turned into months and absolutely no clue of Luther Mitchell. What effects he had at the campsite were gathered up and put into small steamer trunk and sent to his son Ezra. About six months later, an archaeological group set out to dig on an old Indian settlement. One of the people in the archaeological group brought their dog. It was about three days into the dig that the dog could be heard whining in the distance. Someone went to check on the dog and they found a skeleton remains. The skeleton was mostly intact but had been picked of all of the soft tissue and muscle. The skull had a puncture mark, but whether it was a gunshot or the teeth or fangs of some animal was undetermined. The clothing was tattered and ripped, but in a pocket was a small notebook that Luther kept account. On various pages of the notebook were drawings of symbols and a brief explanation of their meaning. The last entry contained the words "Vene, vidi, vici." everyone remembers Caesar's terse account of the Gallic wars. "I came, I saw, I conquered." but no one could understand why Luther Mitchell's body would be located over a mile from his camp site.

"Mr. Haley, was there any investigation of my great-grandfather's death?" Jack was at a loss to give meaning to these facts.

George folded his hands on the table. He took some time before answering the question. He was sure that the answer he had to give Jack Cummings was not going to be adequate. "As far as I know, the death certificate read that Mr. Mitchell had succumbed to the elements and his body had been desecrated by the local animals. There was absolutely no evidence to determine how the hole in the skull had come to be. There was no evidence to give any meaning for the three spent shells in his revolver. When it was all over, my father returned a small trunk that was loaded with small hand tools used for mining."

George made sure he had good eye contact with the young man. "If you take a look at the history of white man's settlement in the Phoenix area you will find all sorts of unexplained mishaps. There are many different theories as there are people. After a while, you just accept the occurrences and move on. My personal belief is the Apache nation may be sequestered on a piece of government reservation land but their gods still own Superstition Mountains."

Jack pulled away from the Haley ranch with a whole new set of question marks. Everyone he talked to was willing to give any information they had. The gaps were filling in, but not with the speed that he deemed satisfactory.

Next stop, the public library and to see what newspaper accounts could do to fill in some gaps. Jack made a mental note to find the map that was linking all of this together.

He pulled into a 7-11 and parked right in front of a public phone. Leafing through the pages of the city offices, Jack found the address of a library a few miles north of the Phoenix city limits, on West Union Hills Ave. Municipal office buildings always had good air conditioning systems. Sitting in the library for a few hours would not be uncomfortable. The heat was clawing at the car windows to get in. No need for the jacket and tie anymore, they were tossed in the back seat.

Jack was right about the library. It was cool, clean, and well lit. Starting at the top of his mental list, Jack decided to see what was documented about treaties between the us government and the native American tribes. There must've been close to 100 different Indian tribes across what would become the United States. Confining it to a geographical area was going to eliminate a lot of wasted effort. Even then, the Indian tribes of the far west were very numerous. The Apache of the South-West have five or six subcultures: Yavapai, Jicarilla, Mescalero, San Carlos, White Mountain and Chiricahua.

The Apaches were given reservation land east of Phoenix Arizona, "Fort Apache Indian Reservation." The government decided that the Superstition Mountains would be held as "Tonto National Park" for the Apache Indian tribe. Jack had read that the Sioux Indian tribe in South Dakota had been given a large tract of land as their reservation. But when gold was discovered on the Indian reservation, the government re-evaluated the reservation size and cut it severely. When oil was found on the remaining reservation land, the government again reduced the size of the reservation. Was it possible that the government was expecting large amounts of gold to be discovered in the Superstition Mountain Range? In addition to living on a reservation, this proud nomadic tribe was forced to become farmers and ranchers. Looking at the land, neither farming nor ranching seemed possible. Stipends of money were to be made available to the Indians to improve their farming/ranching techniques. The distribution of these monies was made by the Department of the Interior/Bureau of Land Management/Bureau of Indian Affairs.

Jack decided it was time to find out about the Peralta family and their involvement with the gold fever that seems to have drenched most of the civilization in and around the Phoenix area. He read about the massacre and the sudden disappearance of gold. Jacob Waltz and the "Lost Dutchman mine" made an entrance into the saga. Jacob would come into the small town of Phoenix with bags of gold nuggets to spend. When he was out of gold, Jacob headed out of town for 2 to 3 weeks and then returns with more bags of gold. Some people decided to follow him into the desert. They never returned. The years were not kind to Jacob. His trips into the desert sapped the life out of his body. Jacob became frail and unsteady in his gait. A lady, Julia Thomas, who owned a sweetshop in the town took Jacob in and tended to his health needs. As Jacob lay dying on a cot, he scribbled a map of the location of his gold mine and gave it to her. When Jacob died, a large store of gold nuggets was found beneath his cot. This served to validate the map.

Julia sold the sweetshop and her home and mounted an expedition into the Superstition Mountains. For over a year

Julia wandered through the mountains. She was not able to find Jacob Weiss' mine. She and the rest in the mining party agreed to give up the quest and returned to Phoenix. Now semi-destitute, Julia would sell copies of the map to anyone with a sense of adventure. The death of Jacob Weiss led to a frenzy of people exploring for "the lost mine." the landscape of the mountains and the connecting Sonoran Desert coupled with unbearable summer heat, many of those with a "sense of adventure" did not return. Mix in the lore of the mountains being sacred to the Apache culture, the rush to make an easy dollar, and the blatant use of a six-gun and a legend appears. Just as potent and perhaps as malevolent as any Grimm fairytale.

Jack sat there for some time, pondering all of this information. The American government had been incredibly cruel to universally all of the Native Americans. If you lived on the East Coast, everyone knew of the "Trail of Tears" and the Cherokee Indians of the Carolinas. The Sioux Indian tribes that lived in the area of the Dakotas had their reservations reduced several times. The Seminole Indians of Florida have never signed a peace treaty with the American government. The military scoured the plains looking for the red man. The Midwest was full of atrocities: Meeker Massacre (1879), The Sand Creek Massacre, Bear River Massacre in Idaho, Wounded Knee Massacre, Gnadenhutten Massacre. The list goes on. Jack felt bad for being a white man. The government banned certain rituals. The legendary ghost dance started a couple of massacres. Indians would only occasionally perform the coming of age ceremonies for the young girls. The US government frowned upon women taking their clothes off and getting high. Eventually, the coming-of-age ceremonies were performed over the Independence Day celebration. The Indians told the Bureau agents that this ceremony was in celebration of the American independence. Jack went on to read that the largest killer of the native Americans was the diseases that the white man brought over. The Indians had no defense for the different bacteria. As a result, whole villages would succumb to the illness and die. No one left to bury the dead. Where was this in the history books? Ah yes, the history was written by white men.

Jack went back to his grand-father's house in a very somber mood. At the dinner table he relayed what he discovered. Rita like Jack had no idea of the atrocities committed. They talked at length of the plight of the red men and what they could do to help relieve the problem. It was well-known that the Bureau of Indian affairs that take the monies allotted to the different tribes and skim off the top for personal finances. There were several tasks the Jack needed to accomplish next day. First, he would look into requirements for a mining claim which he assumed would be controlled by the federal government. Also, he would return to the library and see if there were any interpretations of the markings that were on the map.

Chapter 9

It was a short walk from the parking lot. Plenty of people wandered in and out of a six-story beige colored building. The federal building was in downtown Phoenix. There was a constant switch, swish, swish of the revolving doors behind him as he entered. An anti-chamber greeted him. Two guards, one on either side of the metal detector checked all personnel before they entered. Directions said to put all metallic objects into a plastic tray. Jack put in his keys, wallet, and some change to put in the basket. He exited the metal detector and set off a buzzing sound. A wand from one of the guards showed that all he had a was metal belt buckle. Retrieving all of his personals, he pushed through another door into the lobby of the building. There must've been a 20-degree difference between outside and in the lobby. The huge glass windows were treated to keep out the u-v light and double pane to insulate against the Arizona heat. The click of his heels left a slight echo as he walked across the marble floor.

Two well-groomed ladies were behind the information desk. The lack of people in the lobby made their activity behind the desk seem a bit contrived. Jack asked where he might go to receive information about submitting mining claim. The ladies looked at him with a rather critical eye. It didn't seem right for a man in a dark suit, clean-shaven and with professional manners to be asking about mining claims. He was directed to the fourth floor for the Department of Interior.

Jack walked over to the elevators and observed that no expense was too great for furnishing the lobby of the government building. The Otis elevator was adorned with stained hardwood on the walls. The fourth floor carried the wood paneling throughout the rest of the offices. He was beset by another information desk occupied by an almost identical twin of the girls in the lobby. He again expressed his interest in mining claims and was directed to the Bureau of Land Management. As he walked to the office, the impression of restrained opulence was the design theme.

The secretary for the Bureau of Land Management was a middle-aged woman whose black hair now streaked with some gray was pulled back into a severe bun. The nameplate on the desk identified her as Mrs. Eleanor Sullivan. For the third time, Jack repeated his request. Mrs. Sullivan wrote something on a legal pad and offered Jack a seat in a chair across the room. After several minutes, a door opened and Mr. William Benton strode out to receive Jack Cummings. Mr. Benton was a large fellow a bit taller than Jack and certainly more obese. With a cordial handshake he introduced himself and bid Jack to come into his office.

"Mr. Cummings, welcome! Are you a resident of Phoenix?" William Benton wasn't sure how to accommodate Jack Cummings. He had seen prospectors and miners requesting mining claims to come through his office. Some were grizzled men with straggly beards, soiled pants and shirt and a definite odor. Others came in casual attire, but this fellow before him is in a suit and tie and polished corofam shoes.

"Mr. Benton, good of you to see me. I've been looking through some online documents for the requirements to stake a mining claim and I've found some conflicting passages."

"Mr. Cummings, I can see that you are uninitiated in the rules of mining here in Arizona. There are some basic questions that you'll need to answer in order to submit a claim. Where do you anticipate the claim to be established? If it's on federal land, our office can assist you. If your claim is on Indian reservation land, then you will have to get permission from that tribes elected council. Second, you need to know whether your claim is going to be a mine or you'll be using a sluice box. Will you be using explosives...? How will they be stored? There are OSHA standards that have to be met. Also, there are site inspections to ensure compliance with the standards. You'll have to produce results in order to keep the claim active." William Benton watched Jack Cummings closely to see his reaction. He couldn't find any.

"Can you give me some indication of where your claim might be established? If your claim is in an area of another abandoned claim, we can just renew the previous claim." Benton was trying to politely pump Jack Cummings for some information about the location.

"I have in my possession some papers that describe a mine from long ago. Where the directions on the map would lead me, I have no idea." Jack went on to say, "My grandfather passed away and these papers were found in his effects. I'm following up to see if there is any legitimacy to these old documents."

Jack began to have an uneasy feeling about this encounter with Mr. Benton. All Jack was looking for was the written requirements for establishing a mining claim, and this fellow seemed to be pumping him for information. He didn't like it. William Benton went to a filing cabinet in the back corner of the room and easily pulled out a manila folder.

"Mr. Cummings, here you'll find all the documents to filing a legitimate claim. You say you have a map. If you have a gps locator on your phone, it will make the description for filing much easier. Do you have someone who can act as a guide for you?" Benton was still trying to get information. Jack decided not to even acknowledge the question.

Jack decided to be vague and see if William Benton would continue to pump him for information. "Mr. Benton, you've certainly opened my eyes and I can see that I have a lot of work to do. If I need any explanations, may I avail myself of your services?"

Benton was getting nowhere with this fellow. He thought he would ask one more question and see if this was a real cat and mouse game. "Here is my card," Benton reached for a small box on his wooden desk and produced a calling card. "If you have any difficulties please do not hesitate to call. This area is full of stories and mythical lore. I'm sure you've heard of the Lost Dutchman mine? Plenty of people have been looking for that mine. I'm sorry to say, quite a few have not returned from the desert. You say your grandfather passed away recently. What was his name, perhaps we can send some flowers?"

"Thank you for your concern Mr. Benton, but my grandfather, Ezra Mitchell, passed away last week and has already been buried." Jack didn't think that this would be of any concern. The two men shook hands and Jack left the office with what he had hoped to obtain. William Benton watched the man stride confidently from his office. The encounter had been brief, but definitely was out of the norm for mining claims.

Benton circled his desk and pressed the lever on a small box and asked the secretary to notify Mr. Castellano there was some work for him. As Jack headed down the hall, he pondered the brief sparring with Mr. Benton. He got the distinct impression that Mr. Benton wanted to know all about the map. How many people had come to file a mining claim and had a treasure map in their possession? Not sure where the map would take him, Jack needed to follow up and see what he was up against if it was on Indian property. It was time to return to the library and see what treaties were made with the Apache nation. He made a mental note to check any maps that delineated the boundaries of the Apache reservation. If this went the way he expected, Jack would need a lot of help from Maria.

Chapter 10

Armed with the paper that contained the various markings of the rawhide map, Jack made a leisurely trip back to the library. Late morning activities had only a few souls a library. The sun streamed through the high windows and the air conditioning was already being taxed. Jack found a couple of books on gold prospecting and proceeded to stake out his claim at a long oak table. Fact and fiction intertwined throughout the pages. This was not going to be as easy as he first thought. After over an hour consulting these books, Jack found that more was needed. He climbed to the second floor and searched the racks. As he was about to return to his seat, Jack looked down from the balcony and saw a balding heavyset man bent over his books and scribblings. Jack hurried down the stairs to confront the man but as he came to the oak table, he saw the front door of the library closing behind the man.

"Why would anyone be interested in his notes and scribblings?" Jack rubbed his for head and picked up his various pieces of paper stuff them in his pocket and returned the books. As he left the library, Jack thought of the significant things that occurred to him in the past couple of days. He was assaulted by a pickup on a dirt road on the Apache reservation, and a man interested in his scribblings of map runes. Jack was undecided on his next task and unraveling the tale, the map, and a legend of the Apache gold. After considerable thought, Maria Two Crows could answer a lot of his questions. It was early afternoon and she would be just starting her shift at the restaurant. Good time for a lunch.

He wound through the city traffic and in 30 minutes was at the front of the Apache Junction restaurant. Years of hard sunlight had faded the paint on the small marquee. Jack wandered in and sat at the counter. Two waitresses kept the diner's requests filled. First thing that Jack noticed was the horribly ugly brown skirt and top the waitresses wore. The counter had worn spots in front of each stool. One waitress was picking up an order from the cook, her long black hair braided coming down almost the length of her back. Jack immediately recognized Maria's figure. She loaded the serving tray with various plates of food. One arm balanced the edge of the tray and the other side of the tray rested on her shoulder. She turned to Jack sitting at the counter. A large smile lit up her face. She said that should be right with him as soon as she delivered the order.

"Jack, what a pleasant surprise! I never expected to see you in here." Maria wiped her hands on her apron and leaned across the counter on her elbows. She and Jack were looking eye to eye at each other. Her delight in seeing Jack was obvious. Her dark eyes twinkled and the smile on her face was very genuine.

"What's for lunch, Maria?" Jack wasn't big on afternoon meals, especially on hot days. Maria mentioned that there were some "South of the border" items on the menu. But you had to order mild, medium, or spicy. There was a page on the menu for "Snow Bunnies." This was devoid of a lot of local seasonings and various sauces.

Jack asked what "Snow Bunnies" were? Maria giggled slightly and said it was a local expression for the folks who come here in the winter time to escape the Northern blizzards. She went on to say the tastebuds of these people were "Rather uneducated." He finally settled on a small tossed salad with some salsa and corn tortillas. He pulled out a folded-up paper and spread it out on the table. There was a column of the various different markings, these were all the signs from the rawhide map. He studied the various different definitions that he was able to glean from his research.

Several of the patrons paid their bill and left. Jack thought this an opportune time to mention to Maria his incident in the library. They quietly discussed the issue and who would be interested in Jack's research. Jack hadn't mentioned the map to anyone. As Maria looked down on the paper, she recognized most of the markings.

"You know Jack, even though there have been other maps with similar markings, I think the way we found this map and the manner in which it was made gives some credence to authenticity. If you want, we can take a brief excursion into the mountains and see where these markings direct us." Maria's enthusiasm was up and Jack was beginning to catch some of it also. "Give me a couple of days to get some things together and we can make this an adventure!"

Jack was in good spirits as he left the café. He is going to have to call work and tell them that he would need an additional week or two to get the estate settled. That was sort of true. He decided that there needed to be some pictures taken of the entire map just for security. When he got home, Jack laid out the map on his bed and took a picture with his phone camera. He sat there perusing the different markings burned into the hide. There were a couple of holes in the hide and he rubbed his fingers over a torn piece. A piece of rawhide string used to tie up the map had a small piece of wood knotted into the end and along the length were several small knots. He wasn't sure if there was any significance to these odd additions. He would wait for Maria to come by and they would discuss the significance. He decided that the map had remained unknown in its special hiding place for such a long time, Jack rolled it all back up took it to the workshop and placed it under the oilcloth in the small trunk. He collected all of the old mining tools and set them on top. He slid the trunk back into its original hiding place. A quick inspection and he was satisfied that nothing looked out of place.

Chapter 11

Maria came by the house the next day. Jack retrieved the map from his hiding place and the two of them studied the different signs. Maria noticed that the sign of the sombrero mountain was on the right of the map. On the map, was a symbol for a rising sun and beside it, a symbol for a crescent moon but upside down. These extra markings made the map different from those that were made before. The authenticity of Jack's map seemed real enough. She told Jack she would get the necessary equipment together and she gave Jack the address of the place in the town of Claypool. She said there was an outfitter who could put together all the gear that they might need for a trek into the mountains.

"Jack, you need to wear some old clothes and a pair of high-top boots, like the ones you had on the other day. If you cannot find a bedroll, I can scrounge up one from Granddad's house." Maria came across as rather confident and not at all intimidated by the desert. The sun was beginning to set, and Maria pedaled her bicycle back to her apartment.

Jack went through his notes on the various signs on the map. He rolled up the map again and reset it in the bottom of the trunk. Not much for him to do to get ready. Two fingers of Ezra's whiskey in a glass, Jack and Rita sat on the back patio watching the sunset colors fade into indigo. Rita voiced her concern about this trip into the desert.

"There have been lots of people looking for this silly treasure, and two things have happened. First, no one's found this gold in 160 years, and second there are quite a few people who never came back from the Superstition Mountains. This obsession is what killed your great-grandfather."

Jack took a long sip of the Wild Turkey over ice. He reached out across the chair and put an arm around his mother. "Mom, I don't have any addiction for treasure hunting. But this map that we found is just one of the things that need to be reconciled to bring grandpa Ezra's estate to conclusion. Besides, I get to see Maria quite often." Was there a hint of a smile on Jack's face? As Jack got up, the naked ice cubes clattered in the glass. He leaned over and kissed the top of Rita's head. "Good night, Mom."

It was just after sunrise and Jack was pulling on his grandfather's boots. Rita was in the kitchen busying herself with breakfast. A bedroll lay on the floor beside a cloth bag containing two plastic bottles of water each about 1 liter. Jack wandered into the kitchen as Rita was sliding the bacon onto a plate that already held two sunny-side up eggs. A cup of steaming black coffee completed the breakfast.

"I found the bedroll some time ago when I was rearranging Dad's closet. It's a canvas tarp with a wool blanket inside. The tarp looks pretty beat up. I guess it was used out on the reservation." Rita picked up the bedroll and the bag of water bottles and set them on the table. "Are you sure you want to do this? I never thought of you as being the adventurous outdoors type. There is a hunting knife in a sheath that's in a utility drawer. Would you like to take it along?"

It took Jack a little over an hour to make it to Claypool. He found the outfitter without much difficulty. The sign on the building said, "Happy Trails Tours and Equipment." Maria was sitting in an old wooden chair in the front of the building. Jack parked the car off to the side and pulled the bedroll, the bag with water and grandpa's 8-inch hunting knife. Maria took a close look and approved of everything. She had an old black belt and holster. In the holster, there was an ancient Colt M1911 .45 pistol. She took a look at Jack and smiled.

"You're not going into the desert looking like that! Let's go inside and see if we can't finish your ensemble." Jack was not accustomed to having a woman buy clothes for him. Maria led them over to the clothing rack and pulled off a long sleeve green plaid shirt. She held it up to him but the sleeves were too short. Back to the rack, she finally found one in Jack's size but it was a gaudy red plaid. She went over to the hats and picked out a straw hat. She guessed his size at 7 3/8. She frisbee tossed the hat to Jack. He tried it on and it was a perfect fit. A 3-foot strip of rawhide inserted through the holes on the inside edge of the brim completed the task of a chinstrap. She told him to pick out a pair of leather gloves that were soft and fit his hands. Jack changed shirts in the dressing room and came out with the hat on and the chinstrap knotted.

With this outfit on, Jack had a flashing thought of what a dog must feel like when it's dressed up for Halloween. "I've got spurs that jingle jangle jingle." Jack bent his legs a bit bowlegged, stuck his thumbs inside the top of his pants and sauntered over to Maria. "Golly gee ma'am, where do I pick up my six-gun?" Maria squinted at him and had a big grin on her face.

"Say, cowboy, you new to these parts? Believe it or not, Jack, the long sleeve shirt will keep you from getting sunburned on your arms and keep the sweat close to your body. That hat will help keep you from getting sunstroke and sunburned on your neck. The gloves keep your fingers soft and tender when you get back to that office in Chicago. And, there's no way in hell I'm going to let you have a firearm out here, maybe a big stick?"

All the things got rung up and Jack slid a credit card across the counter. Maria talked to a large barrel-chested man in the corner. Jack just assumed that it was for the rest of the supplies and a truck. She motioned for Jack to head out the back door and she stuck her gloves under her belt. There was a large corral and a couple of smaller outbuildings. Jack looked around for a pickup truck. There was none in sight. He did see a couple of saddled horses tied to a hitching post not far away.

"Maria, I don't see the truck! Did you get one?" Jack was beginning to lose some understanding of what was happening.

"There's your pickup truck. It's just a one-seater." Maria used her chin to point to the horses. "Have you ever ridden a horse before?"

Jack stared at the animals. This wasn't anywhere close to what he had imagined. Horses! What the hell was she thinking? The closest encounter Jack ever had with the horse was when he was at Arlington Park racetrack. It was there, that Jack learned, that fast horses avoided him.

"Maria, I've never been on a horse in my life. I've never even been close to one. I have however been acquainted to several slow ones that took my money. Whatever you have in mind, I hope you know what you're doing, because I am entirely out of my element here." Both he and Maria stood there looking at the animals. Jack thought about his last comment and he wondered to himself, just exactly what was his element.

"Are you afraid of horses? Do they intimidate you? If you are afraid, the horses will sense this and they will make your life hell." Maria started down the wooden steps and confidently strode over to where the two horses and the loaded mule were tied. She walked over to one horse and stood by its head. She took time She moved her arms slowly up to his neck and stroked his mane. "Give the horse the opportunity to smell your scent; this goes a long way for the horse to recognize that you are not a threat. Just copy what you see me do and that will generally keep you out of trouble."

Jack ambled over to the other horse and copied Maria's movements. The horse moved his head around to have Jack scratch his ear, but "Pokey" reached out to take a bite out of Jack's other shoulder. Jack's reactions were fast, but Pokey still managed to tear his brand new shirt. Jack looked over at Maria with a huge question mark on his face. She had seen the whole episode and just shrugged her shoulders. Two hands on the worn saddle horn, left foot in the stirrup and she easily swung the other leg up and over and was astride "Moonbeam."

This whole scenario was counter to Jack's personality. Throughout his life, Jack was in charge and controlled the elements around him. Here was an 800-pound animal that was big enough to do whatever he wanted. Would Maria put him in a position that he couldn't control? He thought, "Jack, you're in charge. How hard could this be?" Left hand grab the reins, both hands grabbed the saddle horn. As he was about to put his left foot into the stirrup, Pokey moved about two steps to the side and Jack's foot was in the air, looking for anything for support. The horse was against the corral fence, the same trick couldn't work twice. Jack tried again with a slowed deliberate mount of the horse and voilà he was sitting in the saddle. A major accomplishment for someone from Chicago.

It was a short briefing on the techniques and posture on horseback. Maria did caution Jack to leave the reins rather loose in his hand as continued tension would only irritate the horse's mouth and if it became calloused, the horse would be difficult to control. Taking the lead rope on the pack mule in one hand, Maria urged Moonbeam around the corral and out of town to the North West. Jack imitated her moves and gave Pokey urging with the heels of his boots. He followed Maria and the pack mule off to the Superstition Mountains. Jack had the same feeling as a 16-year-old kid who parallel parked the family car for the first time.

The fellow in the SUV that was parked outside of the building watched the whole episode. Slowly he got out of the vehicle and wandered into the store. He found the barrel-chested fellow and asked a few questions. He peeled a few bills off of a roll to the fellow and this was an incentive for a few people scurrying about collecting items for a camping trip, on horseback.

Jack and Maria covered 20 miles heading into the setting sun. Jack started out tall in the saddle but after four hours of riding, his shoulders slouched and his head was down. Jack had enough horseback riding for the day. Maria decided to set up camp well before dark to show Jack some of the routine tasks that would be needed for the next couple of days. She picked a level area that was fairly devoid of heavy brush. She had Jack take the lariat and tie a line between two cactuses that were about 8 to 10 feet apart. Each of the horses had a six-foot lead from the halter to the line. Jack watched with some interest as the gear was unloaded from the mule. She took a small nylon tent and inserted some metal rods in various sleeves. The final configuration of the tent was a mini Quonset hut.

Jack set some stones in a circle for a small campfire. Next, he took a hatchet to a manzanita tree. With an armload of wood, it was time for dinner. Maria took some water and cornmeal, mixed them together and made a couple of large tortillas. On an inverted skillet, she put the tortillas to be baked over a hot wood fire. She motioned to Jack to take two of the stones out of the circle that he had put together for the campfire. She told him that this was sandstone and when it got very hot, the moisture in the sandstone would turn to steam and the steam would make the stones explode. Jack was simply amazed at all of the lore that Maria possessed. A half open can of black beans rested on the side of the flat skillet, cooking. A small bottle of hot sauce flavored the beans. When the beans were bubbling in the can, she spread them down the center of both tortillas she folded the ends over and rolled both of the tortillas. Jack was surprised that the tortilla tasted that good. A full day's ride, camping out under the stars, and a basic meal, Jack was quite pleased with himself.

"Maria, I am astounded at your self-confidence and knowledge of this desert. Thank you for showing me ways to survive, and the not treating me like some nimrod."

"Jack, I suspect that if I were in Chicago, you would show me how to survive there. And I suspect you wouldn't want me to have a loaded six-gun there."

As usual, the sun left a brilliant colored sunset to mark the end of day. Maria threw a small handful of coffee grounds into a pot of water. She untied her neckerchief and poured the boiling coffee into a cup, straining the grounds with her red bandanna. As she offered a cup of coffee to Jack, she noticed on a mountain a little over a mile away the glint of the sun off something shiny. Could that have been a pair of binoculars? She smiled. If it was a native Indian following them, that mistake wouldn't have happened. The logical assumption, must be white man. Maria showed Jack some grasses to cut and feed the horses. Darkness settled in in the night sky sparkled with stars.

Maria showed Jack how to set up the saddle as a headrest in the nylon tent. The saddle blanket served as a mattress to soften the ground. The bedroll made the top blanket. Maria held the lantern high and looked very close into Jack's eyes. "Are we going to have a problem in this tent tonight?"

Jack was a bit surprised at Maria's question. His eye squinted together and a bit of a grin was evident. "Ma'am, you have a pistol on your hip, a carbine by your bed, and a hunting knife in your boot. I think I should've asked that question." They both laughed broadly.

This sky was beginning to grow light and Maria was out of the tent. There was wood to be gathered for a fire, a couple of tortillas made, and coffee. Jack followed and did a bit of stretching. Jack assumed responsibility for the fire and Maria made two more tortillas this time she filled them with diced onion and pepper. A couple of armfuls of grasses for the horses and Jack was ready for breakfast. With the sun coming up on the opposite side gorge, Maria knew there would be no more glints from the mountain. Eating utensils all cleaned, the fire was out, and Maria and Jack took the saddles out of the tent. Maria showed him how to place the blanket on the horses back just covering the withers. She showed him how to position the saddle just behind the withers and how to gauge where to tie the cinch strap. She showed him how to use the latigo strap to draw the cinch tight. The bit and bridle were already adjusted to fit the horses. Showing Jack how to put them on was easy. It took the two of them about a half an hour to load the mule with the gear.

Maria asked Jack to take the stones away from the campfire site and to pile them going across the path that they would take when they left. Jack asked Maria what was the meaning of this. Maria said, "The rocks are nice and warm, and in the early morning snakes look for a warm place to sun themselves. Maria wasn't sure if this would work, but it was just an idea. They mounted up and headed up the gulch. Maria looked at the drawings and suggested a way to go that would take them within the site of "Weavers Needle." This was a distinctive rock outcropping that was about 50 feet to 100 feet high. Almost all of the treasure maps had this as a distinctive signpost.

They went about 2 to 3 miles and they heard a couple of gunshots. Maria smiled, said nothing, and urged Moonbeam into a trot. She told Jack that many people had come this way before, all looking for the gold. As they passed certain landmarks, Maria would show them to Jack. In addition, she pointed out old campsites. It seems that Jack's map was one used by everyone who had a desire to explore for gold. They circled around Weaver's Needle and were headed in the direction of Sombrero Mountain.

Maria found a small gully that was protected by a large outcropping of rock. The sun had little opportunity to shine down into the gully and a small pond was able to subsist in the relentless heat. Maria pulled up and checked the water to see if it was palatable. She brought along a small kit that would check the acidity of the water and if there were any biological contaminations. The horses were anxious to drink. Jack slowly got off the horse, his legs and behind were on fire. Maria said to Jack if he could withstand just a couple more hours of ride that they would set up camp early and she had something that she thought would help alleviate his pain. Jack was not going to tell her exactly how much pain he was experiencing. He was glad that he and Pokey had come to a truce. There were times, when Pokey would amble particularly close to a twisted Manzanita tree, in the hopes of brushing Jack out of the saddle.

    Maria directed Jack to cut about an 8-inch strip off his bedroll. She said that if one followed this gully, after several miles it would become a dead end. She said they were being followed and this would be a good way to lose whoever was tailing them. She explained that they would take the animals a couple hundred yards up the meandering gully, then bind their hooves with pieces from the bedroll and they would double back not leaving any trace of the return. Everything went according to plan, and Maria had them take an alternate route. The trail was becoming a bit steeper now and took them East of the Sombrero Mountain.

    At about an hour before sundown, Maria had found a small plateau where they could pitch a tent on some level ground. All the rituals they performed the previous night were repeated again. Only this night, Maria was against making a campfire. Dinner would be a couple pieces of jerky and a few sips of water. Jack reminded Maria of the salve. Maria reached into one of the bags that the mule carried and came out with a small metal can that contained a very strong, pungent brown salve. Jack took the salve over to where the horses were tied and proceeded to drop his pants. Maria meanwhile constructed the nylon tent again. She glanced over the top of the tent and saw Jack rubbing the salve on his bare bottom.

"Nice tight butt," she thought. "But his ass is as white as a full moon." She smiled slightly and continued about pitching the tent. Jack returned with a definite odor, but he seemed a bit more relieved. As they lay in the tent waiting to go to sleep Maria's final words to Jack were, "It smells like I have a mule in the tent."

Jack couldn't resist, "Would you believe, a jackass?"

The next day's activities were a continuation of previous days. Maria and Jack huddled together to look at the map. Their meanderings were going to take them in the direction of the Sombrero Mountain. Maria was sure that she had read the signs properly, but they were tracing paths that people years before them explored. Maria suggested that they follow the map for one more day and if nothing significant appears, call it quits for a while.

John Castellano felt like a fool. He sat there on horseback and looked at the vertical walls ahead of him. There was no way forward. He turned his horse and pack mule around and slowly retraced his steps back down the narrow gully. He wasted the better part of the day and was quite sure he wouldn't be able to find Mr. Cummings and his guide. No need to tell Benton that he was outsmarted by a couple of kids.

Chapter 12

Jack was glad to be sitting in his car, after his intense relationship with Pokey. He decided against more of the disgusting brown salve. When he went to pay the large chested man for the trip, the fellow was aware of the disgusting odor about Jack. He suggested that Jack take a long hot shower immediately upon arriving home. He gave Jack one last piece of advice, "I would put some heavy plastic on the car seat to keep that smell from spreading." There wasn't much to carry back, all the water was gone.

"Come by the house when you can, and we'll go over the map. There's gotta be something that we missed!" These were Jack's parting words as he watched Maria drive the pickup out of sight. He sat behind the wheel for a couple of minutes and pondered his time, out in the desert with Maria. His last thought of her, "What an amazing woman."

Billy Watson was a bit concerned. Maria had borrowed the truck for a few days and Billy was without transportation. The walk to the bar was just a bit of annoyance. What really had him concerned was the fact that he had hidden Maria's dream book behind the bench seat of the truck. If she looked there, Billy's true intentions would come to light and he would have to move out. Of course, the whole reason for him as Maria's roommate/boyfriend was to get a hold that dream book. He remembered what she had said some years earlier about writing down the things that she saw and her dreams. A couple of times she mentioned gold. Could her dream book be just as good as a map? Perhaps the next time she and her new friend would go exploring for treasure he and a couple of fellows from the reservation would trail her and find out what she really knew.

Back at Ezra's house, Rita refused to let Jack into the house. "Take those clothes off and throw them into the laundry. Get a shower and get rid of that God-awful smell." The hot shower soothed all of the muscle pains and washed the salve down the drain. With clean clothes and a tall glass of ice water at the kitchen table, Jack was ready to talk. He recounted all the happenings of the trip into the Sonoran Desert. When he mentioned to Rita his first encounter with horses and the beast's various ploys, Rita first expressed surprise and then she laughed, and laughed. Somehow, the sympathy that Jack was looking for evaporated with the laughter. He mentioned that Maria sensed they were being followed during their trek into the wilderness. He told Rita how easily Maria countered the stalking. He mentioned to his mother that even though his definitions of the map signs were correct, the whole journey seemed mundane. He felt as though lots of people had already come by. The old lady, who had sold copies of a map after Herman Weiss death, had sent people almost on the same trek that he and Maria took. It was reasonable to assume that if all these people before him had come up empty, so would he. He thought perhaps he would go back to the library to look for some more information.

He called Maria who was now working the evening shift at the diner. "You said that there is a map in the Apache Museum that is a copy of Julia Thomas' map that she was selling back in the late 1800s. Can you make a copy of that map and bring it by the house? We'll sit down and compare her map with the one that I have that has been burned into the leather."

The summary that John Castellano provided, told no more than the bare minimum. He monitored the comings and goings of Jack Cummings. Mr. Cummings knew nothing of the lore and life here in the Southwest. In the library he studied the Apache culture, its dealings with the American government and had a cursory overview of the Indian lifestyle. His guide into the desert was a young Apache woman who had a lot of knowledge of desert life. He followed their first sojourn into the Arizona desert, specifically the Superstition Mountain Range. Their trek into the mountains was more or less the same as the other treasure seekers. Nothing looked very promising but he would continue his observation. Mr. Costello traced Maria Two Crows movements to a diner. He walked in and sat at the counter. No one had any suspicions. With a cup of coffee and doughnut, John decided that he would become a regular customer at the diner where the woman worked.

Maria was careful with the map in the Apache Museum. It was drawn on a heavy-duty brown paper. She had to make several changes to the copy machine in order to produce a legible product. With a copy in her purse, Maria pedaled her bicycle over to the Ezra Cummings home. Two blocks away an older car drove slowly and finally passed the house as Maria was putting her bicycle in the backyard. The car drove down to the end of the block made a U-turn and parked under a tree, hidden from the glare of the streetlight.

Jack had the old map laid out on the kitchen table as Maria tapped on the kitchen door. Rita motioned for her to come in and offered some cold bottled water. All three crowded around the table and Maria pulled the copy out of her purse. The elements of the two maps were similar. The relationship of the different signposts was the same on both maps. Both Maria and Jack traced their trip on the large rawhide map. They accounted for the different signs and both maps were virtually identical. Jack plopped himself in the chair and Maria stood there taking a long drink from the bottled water.

"What is it that we're missing?" Jack ran both hands through his hair as he poured over the signs of the two maps. He was completely at a loss for words.

Rita looked at the two maps. "You know what this reminds me of? In the Sunday newspaper, in the comics section, there are two pictures and you are asked to find the 10 differences between the two pictures." Maria and Jack just looked surprised. Back again, they studied the maps in detail. Another hour they spent with a magnifying glass going over everything. Conclusion they came to, the holes in the rawhide map did not show up on the one that Maria had copied. They sat around dejected and looked at the map as if it was written in Greek.

Maria sat down with a sheet of paper. She drew a line down the center and labeled one side "rawhide map" and the other side "map copy." She went down the left side of the rawhide map and any mark that was unaccounted for on the other map she made a note. As she got to the end of the map, there was a small vertical line with the third of a circle and small rays extending out from the circle. It looked like a sign for a sunrise. It was on the bottom right-hand side of the rawhide map and below it was a small crescent. First observation one would think it was a crescent moon. But it was all wrong! The crescent was facing the bottom of the map, upside down. There was no phase of the moon that ever looked like this. All of these things were noted on the piece of paper. Rita wandered over to see what Maria had found.

They both stood looking down at the map and Rita mentioned "Don't forget the holes and that funny looking string tied around the map." And attention was drawn to the long string with several knots and a small peg tied to the end. Jack wandered back and looked at the list. The first item on the list was the partial sun. Jack thought that it was just a piece of decoration and the same for the upside-down crescent moon.

"Jack, what does this look like to you?" Rita's fingers retracing over the burned emblem in the rawhide. "Do you think someone who is burning marks onto the rawhide would put these on as just decoration? I don't think so."

Maria interjected, "At first, I thought it was an emblem of a sunrise. What if it's not a sunrise, but a sunset?"

"But it's on the wrong side of the map! Jack held the map up before him and looked closely at the marking for the sun. "If it's the sunset, it should be on the left-hand side of the map. What we need to do is to look at this in a large mirror. The reflection in the mirror would have the sun as proper sunset marking."

They all hurried into the spare bedroom and Jack held the rawhide map to the mirror. Maria looked hard at the different markings. She wasn't quite sure what to make of this new configuration. Rita stood there with her hand on her chin. As she was looking at this, she wondered out loud, "If the sun is on the wrong side of the map what about the moon? Jack turned the map upside down. That'll put the moon in the proper configuration."

So, Jack took the map and turned it upside down and everyone looked into the mirror. The big question now was, are the markings still valid? Maria took her phone and took a picture of the reflection in the mirror. Then she had Jack turn the map right side up again and she took another picture. "At least we don't have to do this every time we want to study the map."

As Maria looked at the picture of the map with the double reverse, she started to become quite agitated. "Jack, some of these map directions are still valid! The only thing is we're going to be traveling nowhere near where everybody else was. On the original map, we wondered South and West of both Weavers Needle and the Sombrero Mountain. Taking these changes into account, we will be entirely on reservation land. We will be on the other side of Sombrero Mountain. I know for sure that no one has ever done any exploring in this area. You're going to need to get permission from the Apache Reservation Council if you're going to do any rambling through the backcountry of the reservation."

Jack wasn't exactly sure of what he had to say to the Council. Perhaps, they could make some sort of arrangement for division of whatever Jack would find. He knew that he would have to comply with certain cultural traditions to obtain permission. Would he have to do something to placate the kids in that beat-up pickup truck that tried to run him over? He was going to treat this as just another staff meeting. Maria said that she could get the members of the Council together in two days. Jack meanwhile looked at some terrain maps to see what obstacles they had to overcome. He had several questions and decided to drop by Maria's small restaurant to see if she could answer some of the questions. As Jack pulled into the parking lot, he noticed only a couple of cars there.

Sure enough, the restaurant was almost empty. There was a couple at a table and one middle-aged man at the end of the counter. Jack found a seat near the cash register and ordered a cup of coffee and a sweet roll. He asked Maria if they were going to have to take horses into the area they were about to explore. Maria told him that she had not explored this back area of the reservation and had only a rough idea what the terrain was like. Jack pulled out his map and showed her what the official landscape was supposed to be like.

In a quiet voice Maria mentioned to Jack that she didn't think that they should be talking about this in a public place. Jack looked around and mentioned to Maria that there was hardly anyone in the place as it is. Jack glanced down the counter and the fellow at the other end of the counter was working on a piece of pie and a cup of coffee.

"That fella comes in quite often. He says that he is working on inventorying a warehouse a few blocks away. He says he likes to come in here for his lunch break." The fellow was middle-aged, a bit pudgy, thin hair on top and a pair of glasses. Jack took Maria's advice, closed up the map and proceeded to make small talk as he finished his coffee and sweet roll. Jack asked Maria to drop by his grandfather's house at her earliest convenience.

Chapter 13

Billy Watson sat the back end of the bar and was studying Maria's dream book. Maria was a very descriptive writer and Billy had to wade through a lot of her verbiage to get to the parts that were of interest to him. On a separate sheet he made notes. What really upset him was that Maria made no comments about what direction she took. He got through about 20 pages and Maria finally gave them a clue. She mentioned that she flew in the direction of the rising moon. Billy was going to have to do some work now. She has written the date at the beginning of each of her dreams. Billy would have to go back several years and look up that date and the time and direction of moonrise. He felt good this was the first lucky break he got. It was time now to order another beer.

    Otis ambled into the bar and threw a leg over the stool next to Billy. It was a minute or two before anyone said anything. Otis asked him if he had made any headway on deciphering Maria's dream book. Billy slowly shook his head, and said, "She just doesn't put enough detail into her writing. You just can't figure out what direction she is headed. But I think I might have a small clue. I just have to go back a few years and determine the position of the moon." Otis just shook his head.

"Sure is a hell of a lot of work and you don't even know if there's any payoff at the end." Otis pulled a cigarette from the pack, lit it with a match, and deeply inhaled the first draw on the cigarette. It was late afternoon, and the bar was beginning to fill up with customers. A fellow came in and sat on the other side of Billy. He was a chubby fellow with glasses. He ordered a shot of whiskey and small beer as a chaser.

"Howdy boys, name is John." The rest of the evening was casual chat about nothing of consequence. John bought a couple rounds of drinks and everyone departed in a friendly manner. John made a note of the kind of truck that Billy had. He had seen the truck before, but a girl was driving.

Chapter 14

Maria arranged for a tribal council meeting for the following afternoon. Jack asked her to be his mentor. Jack pulled up to Maria's apartment and they drove to the reservation. Maria prepped Jack to not show any emotion. The elders would be looking for any advantage they could get. They would be interested in what kind of mining he was going to use.

Jack was lost in thought for the entire trip. He had no idea what to say to the elders of this Apache reservation. "Let me dig on your land, and I will share what I find." That did not sound like a very persuasive argument. He asked Maria if the elders gathered together very often to determine whether a prospector could come onto the reservation. Maria thought a moment and slowly shook her head. She was trying to recall and nothing was there.

Jack followed Maria's directions to the village of San Carlos and came to stop in the front of a nondescript hut. Several people were standing around outside. Window frames were empty. He stepped inside to a room with three tables side-by-side. Six elders sat behind the tables. Both walls were lined with onlookers. A solitary empty chair faced the council. He slowly looked around the room. All of the occupants were male and Jack concluded that the average age of the men was fifty or better. Every face was the same, wrinkled, weather-beaten, and very serious. The buzz of a single fly was the only sound. He took the chair, and sat with his hands on his knees. Maria wedged herself through the throng of people and stood behind Jack, with a hand on each of his shoulders. She spoke to the Council in the native Apache tongue. She identified herself and said that she would act to interpret the Council's wishes to Jack.

Jack was the first to speak. He told the Council that he was the grandson of Luther Mitchell. He reminded the Council that his grandfather and the Apache clan on this reservation were good friends for many years. He reminded them that his grandfather gave great assistance to those who were raising livestock on the reservation. When his grandfather passed away, it became the duty of Jack Cummings, the oldest male heir, to set straight all affairs of the deceased. He turned his head to Maria, and asked her to repeat his words to the Council in the Apache language. He knew of course that all of the council members understood English language. Maria had counseled him earlier that all Council business must be conducted in the native language of the Apache. This difference to Maria's transcription of his words was a mark of respect to the elders. He continued, that among the papers of his grandfather was a very old map that had indications of gold. Jack said that he had deciphered the markings and concluded that the site of this gold was on the Apache reservation. He was here to ask for official permission from the Apache elders to hunt for the gold. He said that he is willing to share in whatever he should find. Again, Maria translated his request to the elders.

Jack's eyes panned the room. A few people were whispering to each other. As Jack looked at the Council, an older man at the end of the table was looking at him very intently. Jack had expected that the discussion would be about what percentages to divvy up any spoils. One of the elders stood, raised his hand, and spoke to Maria in Apache. He wanted to know where on the Apache reservation he intended to search. When Maria translated the question Jack just shrugged his shoulders and said he wasn't sure. The elders scraped their chairs back from the table and walked single file out of the room. Maria motioned for Jack to get up. They were to leave and the council would deliberate on his request. She said that the Council would have more deliberations with Jack at the rising of the moon tonight. Jack and Maria headed over to her grandfather's house and waited the Council's decision. Jack asked Maria if the Council had ever made this sort of deliberation on someone prospecting for gold on the Apache reservation. Maria said a couple of people had wandered onto the reservation by accident but no one had ever come to the Council requesting approval. She didn't think that there would be any refusal of his request.

It was at sundown and a young man opened the door and motioned for Jack to follow him. Jack took his seat in front of the Council for a second time. One of the elders spoke to Maria for about a minute.

"Jack, the Council is giving you permission to prospect on the reservation. I have been assigned to accompany you and ensure that you keep in accordance with our laws. You can only use pick and shovel. There will be no use of dynamite or sluice box." Maria looked at him for a moment. "Jack, the Council wants 70% of whatever you find."

Jack sat there, frozen by Maria's last comment. He thought that a 50 – 50 divide was very reasonable. Jack raised his hand to make a comment. He told Maria to relay his counteroffer. He asked her to tell the Council that he was in favor of 50 – 50 division. Maria relayed Jack's offer as he watched the faces of the old men. Not one of them showed any sign of recognition. The answer came back immediately, it was 70 – 30 and that was the end of any negotiation. Jack stood without a word, nodded slightly to the men on the Council and backed slowly out of the door.

Maria followed him out the door. He drove slowly away and for several minutes there was silence. "Maria, did you see this coming? I can't believe that they would ask for such a lopsided deal." She just shrugged her shoulders.

"I never thought that they would ask for anything like that. I guess their thinking is, 'We got the gold.' They're just being greedy." She sat for the rest of the trip with her hands folded in her lap. Both were deep in thought.

Jack dropped Maria at her apartment and drove home. He sat at the kitchen table and relayed to his mother all that transpired at the reservation. He shook his head and sipped from a glass of water. "Their idea of negotiation is, 'This is how it will be, take it or leave it.'"

Rita walked over behind Jack's chair and she put both hands on his shoulders. "Jack, the Native Americans have had their lands overrun by whites, air fouled by factory emissions, and prejudices of every sort. When they have the upper hand, I think they are going to take as much advantage as they can."

And Jack thought for a moment. "First things first. Time to see if there is any gold worth talking about." Jack got up, kissed his mother on her forehead and headed off to bed. He still had many things swirling about in the back of his mind. He would get up early the next morning and put in a rugged 5-mile run.

Maria had just finished taking a shower and was combing her long black hair. Billy came into the apartment and was leaning against the bedroom door jamb. The news of Jack's request to the Apache Council had spread quickly. Most of the folks were indifferent. News of a prospector in the Superstition Mountains was a common occurrence. Not many took the time to seek approval from the Apache Council.

"I hear the Council laid a heavy trip on your friend." Billy was trying to keep his interest in the prospecting of Jack Cummings and Maria Two Crows low key. "You know, the Council and its decisions are sort of big news. Are you going to be his guide in this bit of exploration?" Billy was already making plans on how he would follow them in their trek through the wastelands.

Maria didn't want to overplay her hand. She just nodded when Billy asked about her being the guide for Jack's trek into the mountains. "Jack's just the tenderfoot and my big job will be to see that he makes it back from his trek. Whether he finds anything or not I have no idea. He's got some cockamamie map. Frankly, it looks like all the other ones. I suspect he'll be going over a lot of the same area as other prospectors."

"Have you seen his map?" Billy couldn't resist asking.

"Yeah I saw it. We even compared it to that old map in the Apache Museum. That map was made back in the

1850s. They both look pretty much the same. I'm going to bed. See you in the morning." Maria walked off to her bedroom still drying her hair.

Billy had the germ of an idea. He wandered to his bedroom. Lying on his bed, staring at the ceiling, Billy was putting together a plan. Maria just told him that the map Jack had was essentially the same as the map in the museum. He and Otis would have to pay a visit to the museum. A smile lingered on Billy's face as he dosed off.

Chapter 15

Jack spent the next morning going over the map. He was trying to fathom what the holes in the cowhide signified. He made a list of the approximate locations of the holes. He would have to go to the library one more time. The sun was high in the sky by the time he pulled out of the driveway. While Jack was a good driver, he didn't observe the black sedan that had been two cars behind him but mirrored all of his turns. With notepad in hand Jack entered the library, and with a slight wave he acknowledged the librarian.

Two rows of heavy tables were provided for visitors to do any transcriptions or research. At the far end of one row Jack settled with his notepad and pencil. He knew exactly where to go on the second floor. Jack used two buzzwords for his research. The first was "Peralta gold" and the second was "Lost Dutchman Mine." There were several books and a couple of old periodicals. He was looking mostly for descriptions of the landscapes. This was what Jack was good at. He was methodical and thorough. At work, Jack appeared to be slow in his analysis. But he didn't have to go over the documentary material a second time.

It was well beyond lunch when Jack had a hint of what direction he should go. In a couple of books there were references to some adobe tablets. Each of the tablets had some markings impressed on them. He wasn't sure of their significance. It was just another trail he had to pursue. Not sure where they were found, Jack needed a second source to authenticate their location. Jack made a couple copies of the different maps that were in the books and decided to go to the reservation and talk with Maria Two Crows' grandfather. As Jack was putting together material he had gleaned, he remembered his last time in the library and someone interested in his activity. It wouldn't happen again.

It was time for a light lunch. Jack wandered over to the diner where Maria worked. He walked into the diner and noticed a couple of tables occupied and there were three customers at the counter. Looks like Maria was busy. As he sat on this stool at the counter, Jack surveyed the customers and at the end of the counter was that one man who Maria had mentioned was doing an inventory of some warehouse. When Maria noticed Jack sitting at the counter, a smile crept onto her face. There were too many customers for her to act in a personal way.

"What'll you have, sailor?" Maria had poured a glass of ice water and set it in front of him. She had her little receipt book and pencil at the ready. All she could see of Jack was his eyes, just over the top of the menu. She hadn't noticed before, but there were two small wrinkles on either side of his nose. She wasn't sure whether Jack was concentrating on the menu or he was smiling also.

"I believe all have a tuna melt on white toast, with a little mayonnaise and a slice of tomato. Put a glass of ice tea with that also, make it unsweetened."

When she returned with a glass of iced tea and the sandwich, Jack mentioned to her what he had found in his investigations at the library. He asked her if she had ever heard of carved tablets out in the desert.

"Sure, most everybody heard about them. We even have copies of them in our little museum. What you want to know about them?" Maria hustled off to collect a tab that had been left on one of the tables. When she returned, Jack asked her if she knew where these stones were found. She thought for a moment and slowly shook her head. "I don't think anyone remembers that. They were found a long time ago and the stones had been passed around a lot."

Jack said that he would like to talk to her after she got off work. "What time do you get off?"

"I get off at 6:30 this evening. Can we put my bike in the backseat of your car?"

"Not a problem, I'll be by at 6:30." Jack dug a 5 spot out of his wallet and laid it on the counter as he was leaving.

He wandered back to the library. These tablets he decided were a new wrinkle to this very convoluted scheme. Where they come from? Who made them? Did they have any connection with the map that he had? Jack sat and thought more about the stones. Maria had admitted that she did not know where the stones had been found. Perhaps her grandfather could give some insight. Jack spent the rest of the afternoon looking for maps of the Fort Apache reservation. He didn't think there would be much use looking other places.

Jack returned at the appointed time. He walked into the diner and it was three quarters full of patrons. Maria was closing out her till and giving the next girl information on orders that were pending. A slight wave to Jack, and she was out the back door to pick up her bicycle. Jack turned to leave, and he recognized the balding man sitting at the counter. He had a cup of coffee and a piece of apple pie in front of him. Jack walked out and thought it a bit unsettling to see that fellow in the diner so often. Maria's bike was stuck across the backseat and Jack put the air conditioning on as Maria climbed in. They had been driving a couple of minutes and Jack nonchalantly looked down at Maria's feet. She had kicked her shoes off and she was wiggling her toes in the deep pile carpet. The cool air was a great help.

When they arrived at the house, Rita already had dinner on the table. As they sat and ate, Jack thought that there was some connection between the rocks and the map. But he was not sure exactly how things came together. Jack asked Maria, if her grandfather had any idea about where the carved stones had been found. Maria shook her head slightly and said she didn't think her grandfather would know anything.

Jack went to his laptop computer and pulled up a picture of the map. He changed the orientation to accommodate the two reverses everyone decided was required. He magnified the picture several times and it had to be printed off in sections. Not a problem! The individual sections were aligned and taped together.

The Arizona sunset melted and indigo sky dotted with stars took command of the evening. Next to the Ezra's workshop, in the shadows, a man was bent over a strange looking device. It looked like a configuration of small pipes each a bit longer than the one to its left. The pipes coiled around. On a casual inspection one might think it was a series of Pan Flutes. It was pointed at the open sliding glass door on the deck of the house. The coaxial cable connected this configuration to a small black box. Another cable exiting the box with a pair of headphones connected to the man in the shadows.

Jack took a topographical map of the county and laid it beside his printed map. Rita, Maria, and Jack all bent over looking to coordinate any recognizable landmarks. They found Weaver's Needle on both maps and the excitement began. Maria located Sombrero Mountain. The reversal of the map to accommodate the sun and moon symbols correctly indicated a direction completely opposite of where their previous trek had taken them. Jack remarked that the cowhide map while not perfect was a good starting point. He said that there was no need to use the cowhide map any longer and would just return it to the steamer trunk in the morning.

The figure in the shadows turned off the electronic equipment. He gathered together the cable, directional antenna and the black box. He backed slowly out of the property and returned everything to the trunk of his car. He sat in the car till Maria pedaled her bicycle down the street. He drove slowly down the street thinking this should complete his initial report. Mr. William Benton would be interested as to the direction this scenario was taking.

Chapter 16

The next morning, the sun climbed high in the cloudless sky. The temperature at sunup was in this 70° range. By this afternoon, over 100° temperature was not uncommon. Jack started his day as usual with a forty-five minute jog. Rita had a cold cereal breakfast waiting for him when he returned.

"Jack, I found some veterinarian magazines that might be of some interest to Maria. It would be nice if you asked her if she had any interest in them."

He looked up from the bowl of cereal, a small trickle of milk wandered down his chin. "Sure, I can do that. How about early this afternoon after I get out of the library?"

The rolled-up rawhide map lay on the table. Breakfast over, Jack drained the rest of the milk from the bowl. As he rose from the table, he grabbed the map and raised it into the air slightly, showing Rita, and strode out the back door to the workshop. "I'll put this back where it belongs," he said, over his shoulder.

The same fellow from the night before was at the corner of the workshop. Jack unlocked the door and swung on wide open. He rewrapped the map with the oilskin and placed it back in the trunk. The dirty window helped shield the spectator.

By now, Jack had the route to the library memorized. He went to the computer in the library and did a Google on, "Peralta Mine and Clay Tablets." There were several web addresses that had the clay tablets identified. Jack went through each of them and meticulously took notes. The conclusion he came to was, that somewhere from the mid-1940s to the 1950s a fellow by the name Jack Tomlinson came across some tablets that had strange markings. Several people had deduced that these were made by a priest who accompanied the Peralta expedition. On the clay tablets were markings and words that many thought had a connection with the Peralta diggings. These tablets stoked the fires of the prospectors looking for a get rich scheme. There were pictures of the tablets at the end of the dissertation. Jack sat for hours attempting to study and make any significance of them. There was no outward connection between the markings on the tablets, Jacob Weiss' Lost Dutchman Mine, and the Peralta Mines.

It was about lunchtime when Jack decided to go see Maria. The parking lot to the diner was about half full. Jack walked in and his seat at the counter was empty. Maria came out from the waitress pickup station with a large tray filled with orders. She saw Jack as she came out and as he passed, she whispered, "I'll be with you in a few moments."

He pulled a large menu card from a holder and pretended to scan it. He let his eyes wander to the top of the menu and there at the end of the counter was that same fellow, with coffee and pie. Maria came by with a glass of ice water and had her pad out to take his order. Jack asked her if the pie and coffee fellow had any conversations with her. Maria said that all he did a, was places order and took his own sweet time finishing it when it came. No small talk. Jack ordered his usual sandwich and this time asked if they had any dill pickles.

When she placed the sandwich and dill pickle spear in front of him, Jack asked her if she would like any of the veterinarian magazines that had collected at his father's house. He wasn't sure what they contain, but perhaps there would be some procedures defined to give her some additional insight. Maria told Jack that he could drop the magazines by any time he was free. He could just put them inside the vestibule door and she would pick them up when she got off shift.

As Maria was totaling up the bill, Jack summoned up the courage. "Would you like to go out with me, for dinner?" She quit scribbling on the bill and just looked at him. It took about 4 or 5 seconds, but Jack was sure it was much longer than that.

"Sure. You have any ideas where to go? Want to go somewhere fancy, or casual?"

Jack thought a moment. "I think casual would be easier on both of us. You know of any Italian restaurants in town?"

Maria said that she knew of a couple places. Jack could pick her up at 7 PM tonight. That was easier than he had thought it would be. With the bill paid, Jack wandered back to his grandfather's house. He figured he'd take a shower and change into some more comfortable clothes.

Jack pulled up to the front steps of Maria's apartment building. She said her apartment was on the fourth floor, apartment 4F. The hallways were clean, but age had taken its toll. The colors were faded and the floorboards creaked. He knocked on the door and Billy Watson answered the door. Billy and Jack locked eyes briefly.

"Hi, I'm Jack Cummings and I'm here to see Maria." Jack thought to himself briefly, 'what's Maria's last name?' Billy stood back and motioned for Jack to come in.

"You got a date with Maria?" Billy slid into an overstuffed chair that had seen years of heavy use. He lit a cigarette and reached to the coffee table for an open can of beer.

"It seems Maria and my grandfather were associated to provide veterinary care to the livestock on the reservation. My grandfather died just recently and left a lot of his medical equipment to Maria. We became acquainted over the past couple of weeks." Jack didn't think that he should give Billy any more information than that. Billy's social graces didn't give Jack any incentive for more conversation. He stood off to one side and waited for Maria to appear.

She appeared in the doorway, bedroom. He had never seen Maria in a dress before. The dress was light gray and had diagonal streaks of silver and iridescent blue. One side of the dress was about a foot longer than the other side. The 3-inch heels put her eye to eye with Jack. Black curls of hair rested on her shoulders. Her dark eyes were highlighted with a hint of blue eyeshadow. While she had red lipstick, the color was subdued, kind of smoky.

Jack cleared his throat, "I thought you said casual?"

Maria smiled broadly, "You saw what I have to wear at that diner, and the hair has to be tied back also. I don't get much of a chance to kick my heels up. I can change if you feel ill at ease?"

"No! I wouldn't dream of taking you out in that waitress uniform. What kind of restaurant did you have in mind?"

"It's a nice Italian restaurant, a bit sophisticated. I think it would be something that you would be comfortable with in Chicago."

With Maria providing the turns, Jack spent a half-hour driving and they ended up at "Uncle Sal's Market." Maria had made reservations. They both were immediately seated at their table. The surroundings were chic and Maria was not overdressed. As they were seated at their table Maria leaned over and whispered in Jack's ear, "I do not drink anything with alcohol." Jack smiled at Maria and just nodded. When the waitress came by for drink orders Jack ordered two virgin daiquiris. The menu had various pasta dishes available and if you ordered something that was meat, you also got a side of spaghetti.

Jack was pleasantly surprised with the change in Maria's demeanor. During the day, she was pretty much all business and hard logic. But in the evening and dressed very sophisticated, Maria presented another side. In addition to being alert and oriented to her surroundings, Maria had a delightful wit. They talked about the stone tablets and if they had any connection to the treasure map. Maria said she had the next day off. Jack invited her to drop by and look at the veterinary magazines for articles she might think important. Maria volunteered to put together a second camping expedition. Jack asked her if there were any places in town that sold "butt protectors for beginning horseback riders." They took over two hours for the meal. Jack asked her if she would like to go dancing in the city. Maria knew of several places to go dancing, depending upon style of music.

She begged off, telling Jack, "Tonight's not a good night for me to go dancing. I've been on my feet all day at the diner. Perhaps we could plan this for another evening?" Jack thought about this a moment and decided that this was the most delightful way of being turned down. She left the possibility open of another date. It was close to 10 o'clock when Jack pulled up in front of Maria's apartment building. He was out of the car in a flash, one hand holding her car door open the other reaching in to offer support.

Maria took a second to look at Jack's hand, offering to help her out of the car. A sneaky smile appeared on her face as she used the hand to steady herself as she swung her legs out. In the heels, she and Jack were eye to eye. She held onto his hand as he walked her over to the flight of stairs.

"This is been a wonderful evening for me. I guess this dumb job takes up a lot of my time." Maria's dark eyes looked intently into Jack's blue ones. That second of quiet pause made an indelible mark. They were standing close, and Maria put one hand on each of Jack's cheeks. She pulled him in and gave him a gentle kiss. The evening air was cooling, but Jack felt like his body had been jabbed by 10,000 scorching hot pins. He stood transfixed, as he watched the sway of her hips as she climbed the concrete steps. She unlocked the vestibule door, and as she went inside, she turned to look at Jack and gave him a warm smile.

Chapter 17

Jack put the rental car into gear and slowly steered back to Ezra's house. Moments later, a pair of headlights turned on and pulled out into traffic behind Jack's car. John Castellano eased his car out onto the road and decided to call it a night. He would put his notes together for his meeting with Mr. Benton tomorrow.

John Castellano had been doing surveillance for several years. Most of the times, it was some nimrod from out of town or out of state with a map that guarantees untold riches. Most of the maps were the same and you could tell how the person handled themselves coping with the Arizona heat.

Back in the day, when Jacob Weiss had found a vein of gold, people would follow him into the desert. Not many were able to return. But Jacob would return with small sacks full of pure nuggets. Jacob had a good time until the nuggets run out. He would leave Phoenix for three or four weeks and the cycle would begin again. In 1890, Jacob

Weiss' health began to fail and he was ministered to by a woman named Julia Thomas. Julia owned a confectionery shop in the town of Phoenix. On his deathbed, Jacob scribbled out a map to show where his gold mine was located. After Jacob died, Julia sold her store and mounted an expedition to find the mine, but after several months in the Superstition Mountains she was not able to find it. She returned to town, penniless. She was able to sell copies of Jacob Waltz map to make her ends meet. The lore about the "Lost Dutchman Mine" built over the years. The Superstition Mountains kept its secrets for 150 years.

It was late morning when Maria dropped by Jack and Rita's home. Rita had coffee and some homemade biscuits to offer. Jack pulled out about 20 magazines on veterinary science. He had copies of Journal of Veterinary Medical Education, Veterinary Medicine, and Veterinary Parasitology: Regional Studies and Report. Maria could go through the tables of contents and pick out which periodical was of interest. Jack was more concerned with the maps and where their next treasure hunt would take them. He correlated his treasure maps with overhead photography of the Apache reservation. There were no roads to be found and vegetation was very minimal.

Maria had Scotch-taped the different sections of the map together to produce one that had the landmarks with the corrections. They both agreed their path would take them along the landmark that indicated there was a stream. They would have to cross the stream and proceed almost in a Northern direction. Jack figured that the distance they covered would be approximately the same amount as their last expedition. It would be 3 or 4 days out and 1 to 2 days back. The whole excursion would be approximately 4 to 6 days.

"Jack, you think you can ride for 6 days straight?"

He shrugged his shoulders, "Guess I'm gonna learn really fast."

Maria got the telephone number of the Happy Trails Tours and Equipment. She rattled off her requirements and added additional feed for the horses. The food that she asked for, consisted of a couple of cans of beans, some fresh onions, corn tortillas, and about 3 pounds of jerked meat. She turned and gave a thumbs up sign to Jack and his mother.

"Jack, they want to talk to you. You gotta give them your credit card number." Maria was pleased with herself that this is excursion could be planned on such short notice.

Maria said that she had to go and pack her gear for the trip tomorrow. She told Jack to meet her at sunup and they would get an early start on the day. Jack decided to do some shopping of his own. He had seen a Western outfit store on the main drag going through Tempe. He'd stop by and see if they had anything to help the neophyte horse person. He wondered if he should ask if they sold any handguns. Jack had this infatuation with having a 6-gun strapped to his hip. After all, he had the boots and the cowboy hat.

The next morning, as the Eastern horizon showed glimmers of light, Jack packed his gear in the trunk of the car. Rita made Jack a quick breakfast of some scrambled eggs on a slice of toast and a cup of coffee. As the Eastern sky lit up in earnest, Jack slid the car out of the driveway and was off to Maria's apartment. It took him only 15 minutes to make it to her apartment building. Traffic was almost nonexistent this early in the day. He pulled up to the front steps of the building and could see Maria sitting on the steps with a couple of bags in front of her.

It didn't take long for them to get out of the city. Rush-hour traffic had started, and it was going to be in the opposite direction anyway. After an hour or so, the village of Claypool showed up in the distance. Jack swung into the parking lot and pulled his car off to one side. It was gonna be here for a few days, no need to hoard the prime parking spots. Even though the hour was early, the building was lit and an Open sign hung on the front door. Jack volunteered to take both knapsacks and a large laundry bag filled with things that clattered. There was a porch that ran around 3 sides of the building, the 4th side set up to accommodate semi's with trailers. He sat in a wooden chair, waiting for Maria to complete whatever paperwork was needed.

Just like the last time he was here, 2 horses and a loaded mule were tied to the corral. Jack looked really hard to find out if these were the same animals that he had at their last excursion. The only thing he could ascertain, was, they were the same dark colors as the previous animals, and they had 4 legs. Jack reminded himself as he sat there, "Be sure to ask Maria if she brought that ungodly grease with her."

As Maria came out the back entrance of the store, she gave Jack a thumbs up. She grabbed her knapsack and the laundry bag and headed to the horses. The backpack was secured behind the saddle and the laundry bag tied in with the rest of the supplies on the mule. She spent a minute with the horse, inspecting the saddle, the length of the stirrups, and the tightness of the cinch. She motioned for Jack to do the same. Her left foot into the stirrup, Maria grabbed the horn and swung easily into the saddle. Jack mimicked her motions, and soon was sitting atop a black horse.

As they wandered around the corral and to the northeast, Jack caught up with Maria and asked her, "Do these horses have a name?"

"I'm riding Lollipop. And I believe, you've got Satan."

Jack thought to himself as they meandered into the rising sun, "This trip is not starting out the way I expected."

They put a good number of miles behind them as the sun settled over the Western mountain peaks. Surprisingly, Jack felt a lot better at the end of the day's ride than he did on their last excursion into the desert. For almost half a day the terrain they covered was a slight uphill grade. Vegetation was becoming sparse and the ground was becoming nothing but slate.

Maria was looking around for suitable campsite when she noticed, the mule had picked up a stone in its hoof. She dismounted and took a hoof-pick from one of the saddlebags. She moved close to the head of the mule, patted his neck and let him smell her. Maria moved her hands down the front leg of the mule and she leaned slightly into the animal. She pulled up the leg and inspected the underside of the hoof. Sure enough, wedged in between the horseshoe and the "frog" was a stone. The hoof pick resembled a screwdriver where the last 3 inches of the shaft was bent at 90°. She used it to dig in and remove the stone and any other debris the that may have collected. She decided to check all three animals to make sure it that no other hoofs had the same problem.

"You know your way around horses," Jack commented as he watched.

"This looks like a decent place to camp." Maria pulled the tent from the mule and started to assemble it. "I learned that stuff when I was a little girl. It's something that is almost unconscious for me. The terrain in this part of the country is very severe and if horseback is your only means of transportation, you pay attention to the animal's well-being. If you check your car for gas, oil, water, and tires your chances of being stuck out in the desert are greatly reduced."

As the sun was going down, Jack made the traditional campfire. Maria took a small amount of water, put it in a pan, added some beans and beef jerky and onion. While the concoction was coming to a simmer, Maria worked some cornmeal and a small amount of water together and made a couple of large tortillas. An upside-down skillet over the fire was perfect to fry up the tortillas. Jack stirred the beans and jerky and pronounced it ready to serve. It was the perfect filling for the tortilla. Dinner was simple, quick, and only one pan to clean.

She motioned Jack over to the animals. I'm going to show you how to curry and brush the animals. In the saddle bag was a stiff bristled brush and a "currycomb." Jack thought that the currycomb was nothing more than a large back scratcher. He watched as Maria attended to her horse, Lollipop. It took about ten or fifteen minutes and she tossed the two implements to Jack. He did the same thing to Satan. Both horses responded well and seemed to show an appreciation for the attention they were getting.

"Jack, the animals respond well to this attention. The horses are more relaxed and know that the human can be trusted. It gives us an opportunity to see if the gear and saddle have been well positioned and not chafing the animal."

Jack put a couple of pieces of dead manzanita on the fire. The flames should stay small and provide some hot embers at sunup. He climbed into the tent and zipped it shut. Maria was in her sleeping bag and as usual, armed to the teeth. In the darkness, the moon rose to give an eerie light to the desert. Jack was just about to go to sleep, when Maria put her hand on his arm.

She whispered to Jack, "Listen! Can you hear it? I think that's beautiful." Far in the distance was the sound of a coyote howling at the moon. "Jack listen! They're singing to us! Now wait for a moment and you'll hear a reply." And sure enough after a couple of minutes, from somewhere even farther away was a faint response.

He lay there in the darkness, drinking in the faraway sounds that broke the stillness. Maria's sensitivity opened a door for him. Jack smiled into the darkness and wiggled his butt down into the sleeping bag. Maria lay there close beside him. Was she awake? As he drifted off to sleep, his breathing slowed and became much deeper. He recognized a different fragrance. He thought it might be perfume. Was that Maria? His last thought was the movie, "Scent of a Woman."

About a mile South of Jack and Maria's camp, another camp was being made. John Castellano was rather accomplished at making a campsite. He had been working for the director of Bureau of Land Management for a few years. His job was to follow and report on the nimrods who had some kind of treasure map, bent on finding the Lost Dutchman mine. John like to keep his supplies to a minimum. Canned goods supplied the bulk of his food. He had a small one burner gas stove that worked quite nicely heating his canned meals. What he liked best about the little stove, was, it didn't give off very much light.

The next morning came all too quickly. The sun rose in the sky with a vengeance heat against all that survived the night. Not a cloud to be seen anywhere to the horizon that could mitigate the sun's intensity. Maria was already up and had a large water bag that she used to fill the canvas feed bag for the horses. The bag could hold approximately a gallon of water that she only filled it halfway. There were breathing vents along the sides of the bag and could be zipped open or closed depending upon what was in the bag.

The temperatures yesterday, had tickled 100° mark. Today was starting out to be exactly the same. Maria looked at the bags of water and wasn't quite sure if there would be an adequate amount for her and Jack and the animals. Perhaps this stream that they had to cross would help.

Joe Castellano struck his meager campsite and had a can of Spam for breakfast. A quick look North through the binoculars, showed a small plume of dust. He took off his beat-up old hat and filled it with water from a larger jug. He watered his horse and the mule. Joe was sure that this would not be enough water to get through the day. No need to be in a hurry today. Joe felt very confident that Jack and Maria were not aware they were being followed. His small butane grill did not emit much light when he made camp. He just had to keep his own dust plume to a minimum.

The sun reached its zenith in the cloudless sky. Jack and Maria urged the horses on at a leisurely pace, keeping the Sombrero Mountain off their left shoulder. It was a long, slow track, always on a slight uphill incline. Vegetation was becoming sparse and you could hear the clip – clop of the horses' hooves on hard rock. Jack had drank a little more than half of his canteen and it was barely noon time.

Maria pulled to a halt, and gazed around at the hills and the skyline. From a saddlebag she retrieved the map. Jack pulled up beside her and they both studied the markings. Maria estimated that they were just a few miles from a creek. Jack looked about and surveyed the landscape. He figured if there was vegetation there should be some tall trees. There was not one to be seen. Maria pointed out the direction they would take. With her heels, she urged Lollipop forward.

Joe had been sitting some distance away and his binoculars took in all of Maria and Jack's pause. It gave him a warm feeling, when he saw her point to something in the distance. At least he knew the general direction they were headed. He didn't have to keep them in view all the time. He just had to be very observant when they made camp.

It was early afternoon when Jack and Maria came upon a gorge. It was approximately 30 foot in width and 70 to 80 feet in depth. Jack got off the horse and went to the edge to look down. He could see a fast running creek at the bottom of this.

"Maria, you think this is the creek that's on the map? If we have to get across this to continue our trek, I think this is a showstopper."

"I gotta tell you Jack, I've never come upon this before. In fact, I don't think anyone on the reservation is been to this part in a very long time. Let's just ride along the gorge and maybe we'll come to some kind of bridge."

They both climbed back into the saddle and set out at a brisk pace. The gorge was in a North-South direction and the sun would only shine to the bottom of the chasm in the noontime hour. It took a couple of hours and they finally found a footbridge that spanned the gorge.

Maria dismounted Lollipop and tied her to a post that was set into the ground to help hold the footbridge. Holding onto the ropes on either side she walked out onto the bridge and tested its strength. She encountered very little swaying in the wooden slats looked thick enough to carry considerable weight. Jack sat slouched in the saddle. He had a wholesome fear of heights, and this was just about all he can handle.

"Do you plan on going out on that?" Jack's imagination reeled all sorts of scenarios. None of them ended with him and the horses on the other side. "How the hell are we going to get the horses across that?"

"Jack, don't worry. I've looked at the bridge and I can see where animals have been taken across by the marks their hooves made in the wooden slats. Are you afraid of heights? You know that skyscrapers in New York City in Chicago were built by Indians. For whatever reason, Indians don't have a fear of heights." Maria smiled broadly at him and motioned for him to join her.

She looked around for some material to cover the horse's eyes. And whatever she found was either too large or too small. She hesitated for a moment, look straight at Jack and unbuttoned her long sleeve shirt and took it off. Jack stood transfixed. He wasn't quite sure if he should say something or acknowledge the marvelous figure that Maria had. He decided to say nothing and treat this as the logical solution to a small problem. She let the back of the shirt drape over the horse's eyes and she tied the arms underneath the horse's neck. She took some time with the horse. She patted the horse's neck and rubbed it. She let the horse get a good whiff of her scent. With the reins, she encouraged the horse to come to her and she walked backwards over the narrow footbridge. Lollipop came haltingly at first unable to assess the new feeling. Hardly any swaying occurred and the horse walked comfortably across to the other side. Maria tied the horse to a retaining post on the other side and came back to get the mule. Maria took extra time with the mule and did her best to make it feel comfortable. She repeated the procedure and the crossing was without incident.

Jack stood there beside Satan wondering how this was going to turn out. Maria came back and tied the shirt over Satan's eyes. "I'll take care of this. There's no need for you to get involved. Besides, it's your turn to get across." Maria smiled. "Jack, I have a question. Do I need to get another shirt and tie it over your eyes?"

Jack walked onto the wooden slats, both hands on the guide ropes. As he stepped out onto the slats, he could feel the breeze. Just him, a wooden bridge, and nothing but air. He made a concerted effort to keep his eyes on the post on the other side of the bridge. He thought it was an eternity to get to the other side. But when he put his feet back on the ground, he was truly thankful. Maria followed behind with Satan blindfolded. The horse acted as if he had done this several times a day. He almost trotted across with Maria trying to stay out of his way.

"Jack, did it bother you that I took my shirt off?" Maria finished buttoning her shirt on.

"It did startle me a bit at first. But any thoughts of semi-naked women were completely driven out of my mind with my second step onto the footbridge. I find it almost impossible to think lurid thoughts when I'm swinging 70 to 80 feet in the air." Jack smiled broadly. They both mounted up and the trek continued its leisurely pace.

It was about an hour and a half later that John Castellano came upon the footbridge. He sat there looking at the footbridge, not quite sure what to do. He pulled the hat off his head and used his sleeve to wipe the sweat. "They made it across, dammit. How did they do that?" He figured he better take one animal at a time across but he wasn't too sure if the animal would rebel at the height. He tied up the pack mule at a post and gingerly walked his horse out onto the wooden slats. It seemed that the horse didn't mind the bridge or the altitude at all. With the horse tied at the other end of the footbridge he went back for the pack mule. As he led the pack mule up to the footbridge the mule was determined that he was not going across that abyss. He stopped several feet short and as Castellano pulled on the reins the mule bayed in protest. And no matter the encouragement, this mule was not going across that footbridge! John went into the gear that the mule was carrying and pulled out a cloth that he used to wipe his mess kit. He tied it over the mule's eyes and gingerly walked the animal across the bridge.

John sort of felt sorry for the mule. He wasn't particularly enthused about walking across the footbridge himself. As he was just coming up to the other side of the footbridge, he thought about that old saying, "Out of sight, out of mind!" He took out his binoculars and panned their horizon to see if Jack and Maria were still in sight. Nothing to be seen!

Jack and Maria meandered along the chasm still heading north. The hot sun baked just about everything in sight. All the water bottles were about three quarters empty. As they took a break to rest the horses, Jack came up with an idea.

"Do we have any sort of bucket that we can use to get water that's at the bottom of that huge gully? Perhaps we can tie something on the end of the rope and refill the water." Maria thought that was a great idea. She dug into the pack that the mule carried. She found the feed bag that she put grain for the horses and mule. It was made out of heavy canvas. No reason, why it couldn't hold water also.

They took the horses close to the edge of the cliff and tied to a manzanita tree. Maria took the lasso from her saddle and threw the end of it over the cliff to see if it was long enough. No such luck. She took the lasso from Jack's saddle and tied the two together. With the bag tied to one end it was lowered over the side and down into the gully. The retrieval went without a hitch and there was approximately a gallon and one half of water.

Maria pulled out a test kit and checked the water. According to the color chart the water registered with the pH of 7.4, slightly basic. She conducted another test to determine if there was any organic material in the water. She inserted a small tablet into a vial, filled with water and put a cap. She shook it vigorously and set it on the ground.

"This is just a rough test to see if there is organic material in the water. You know, if something is either growing or decomposing. It measures the amount of oxygen. It will take five minutes." Maria inserted the strip of something into the vial and it turned the light blue.

"Wow! This water is almost perfect!" She poured the water out of her canteen and refilled it with the water from the feed bag. She took a healthy drink and just smiled. "Let's get the animals watered first."

Jack pulled out all the other water jugs and use them to fill one completely. He waited for his turn to fill the other jugs. Maria looked at the position of the sun and suggested to Jack that they look for a place to camp for the night.

They headed away from the creek and came upon a place where the rock extended some 8 to 10 feet above them. Maria gave him a thumbs up and proceeded to dismount and set up the tent for the night. Jack's usual chore was to center a ring of stones and go look for firewood. Small manzanita trees littered the surrounding area. He came back for the huge armload and saw that Maria had the tent erected and the two horses and mule were tied to a makeshift line.

Jack set up the campfire to be close to the rock wall. He figured that the heat from the fire will reflect off the wall and keep them warm till at least when the fire went out. Maria kept a casual eye on Jack as she was setting up camp. She was surprised at the ease with which Jack adapted to living in the wild. Jack said that he was going to go out and collect some grasses for the animals. Maria cautioned him to look out for "locoweed." She said the easiest way would be to only find grasses with long stems and to collect weeds where the leaves were broad. She said, "In general locoweed looks like endive."

Maria emptied two cans of Dinty Moore beef into the small pot and hung it over the fire. She proceeded to make two large tortillas as the sun was sinking over the mountain range.

The horses were tied to a line that was secured around two large boulders. Jack had an armload of grasses for each of them. The sun was gone from the horizon but a line of orange sky outlined the horizon. Jack and Maria set up their bed rolls. A breeze sprung up and Jack decided to use the saddle blanket on top of his sleeping bag. Maria left the entrance to the tent open and thrown back. The heat from the fire bounced off the small rock cliff and into the tent. The camping routine was well practiced.

They been asleep about two or three hours when the horses began pawing at the dirt and making short nervous neighs. Jack awoke and heard the commotion. Quickly out of the sleeping bag, he crawled to the entrance of the tent still clutching at his saddle blanket. The commotion pulled Maria from a sound sleep and she was right behind him.

As Jack just crawled out from the tent, the quiet of the night was shredded with an animal scream. Jack turned in the direction of the sound. It came from a plateau not 6 feet above their camp. Crouched above him was a large cougar. Jack could see his yellowish orange eyes in the moonlight. His ears laid back flat, and his mouth open to show his fangs. A second scream tore into the night air. The horses tied underneath the small outcropping of rock were prancing, clawing, pawing at the dirt. Their heads held back, eyes wide with fear. The cat saw no reason to keep from attacking one of the horses. With deliberateness the cat picked his prey.

Jack came around the corner of the tent and raised his saddle blanket high. With a loud, "Haye," he got the attention of the cat. The yellowed eyes turned and sized up the newest victim. The blanket showed his adversary to be very large. Were there claws? Any fangs? The cat turned to a new prey. The muscles tensed and rippled along the cat's shoulders, waiting for the perfect timing.

Maria came out of the tent and saw the cat on the ledge. She unholstered the ancient pistol and tried to draw a bead on the cat but Jack was in the way. She saw the cat turning to make Jack its new victim. She had to do something! She raised the gun into the air and fired a shot. The mountain lion tensed. She immediately fired a second shot and that seemed to do the trick. The lion turned quickly ran into the darkness. Jack had jumped at the explosion just behind him. Then a second shot rang out, he felt as though thousands of pins pricking his skin all over his body.

Maria walked over to the horses and patted each one on the neck and let the horse smell her scent. The horses look like they had settled down, but you could see their eyes moving back and forth ever on the alert. Jack walked over and help calm one of the horses.

"I think you saved my life. But that pistol shot right behind me scared me out of about five years growth." You could tell Jack was relieved, he was starting to make smartass remarks.

Maria felt relieved how the situation resolved. "I'm glad it ended the way it did, I really didn't want to shoot such a beautiful animal." Jack turned and looked at her as if she had said some incredible off-color word. "Well the 'ndolkah' was just looking for food. I'm sorry, that's Apache for cougar. Jack, I'm sorry to tell you this, but out here, you're not at the top of the food chain."

Jack mumbled something as he crawled back into the tent. Maria asked him to repeat himself. Jack replied with, "What makes you think living in Chicago put you at the top of the food chain?"

John Castellano was asleep in his small tent but a distant gunshot awakened him. There was a second report. John sort of smiled into the darkness. "Nothing like roughing it when your camping." With that last thought, John went back to sleep.

The next morning arrived cloudless and hot. Maria was poking through the ashes of last night to find some hot coals. Jack unzipped the sleeping bag, rolled out to the side and crawled out of the tent. He picked up some pieces of manzanita and help to get a small fire started for breakfast.

Maria took some of the water and mixed it with some sort of flour. She took some of the jerky, pulled it apart and put it into the skillet to fry. The flour mixture was poured over the jerky. Jack watched with amazement as she took her hunting knife and loosened the bottom of the concoction. She swirled the pan once or twice to ensure this huge pancake was free. And with the deft flick of the pan, she had it turnover in the air and land back in the pan. As she put the pan back on the fire, she looked up at Jack and just smiled.

"Jack, are you wearing that medicine pouch that my father made up for you?"

"Well yeah," he stammered. "Your dad said that I should wear this every time I was on the reservation. Is there something wrong?"

"I had a dream last night and it upset me."

Jack asked, "Did it have anything to do with the cougar that visited our campsite last night?"

"I don't think so. It was similar to one of those dreams I had when I was younger. In my dreams, I would imagine that I am a crow flying somewhere. I'm usually flying towards something. But last night's dream was different. I was flying towards a canyon, and as I got close to it, I would veer away. This happened several times in the dream. I don't have any idea what it means."

They both munched silently on their "pancake." Each wondering what the day had to offer. Each horse took a turn at the feed bag to get a drink of water. Maria saddled the horses as Jack collapsed the tent and packed everything away on the mule.

They proceeded in a northerly direction, the horses at a slow walk. A slight incline in the terrain was a reminder that the Superstition Mountains would soon make itself known.

About a mile and a half behind Jack and Maria was their shadow, John Castellano. He performed all the same tasks that Maria and Jack had accomplished. Through the binoculars he could barely make out their forms. The rock formations were flat and vegetation very sparse. He observed that they still kept a Northerly direction in their trek. For a pudgy older man, John swung easily into the saddle. With a couple of wraps around the saddle horn, the lead rope to the supply mule was secured. A slight urging of his heels into the horse's flanks, John and his two four-footed companions headed into a leisurely Northern direction. He had followed other nimrods out into the desert, but none of them had ever gone over this piece of land.

John and Maria had been in the saddle about three or four hours. The landscape had not changed much since they broke camp. It was a gentle uphill cant, with dark magenta rock. Hardly any vegetation impeded their progress. Maria reined her horse and the pack mule to a stop. She pulled one boot out of the stirrup and swung her leg around the saddle horn. She was sitting almost sidesaddle and looked very comfortable. Satan clip-clopped with Jack astride in the saddle up beside Maria.

"Jack will you pull out the map. We can get our bearings. There is not much here to give us any indication how we are heading."

The folded-up map was four sheets of paper Scotch taped together. Jack pulled the map out of the saddle bag, stretched it out and handed it to Maria. The last indicator on the map, was that pristine creek that they passed almost 2 days ago. Maria checked against one of the sign posts. Sombrero Mountain was visible from most every place on the map. Maria made it a point to keep the Sombrero Mountain off her left shoulder. As she looked out to the horizon, she could see an easy path through what appeared to be a gulch or canyon. The map did not give any indication what direction to take. Jack and Maria had no idea of how close they were to the Peralta mines. A choice needed to be made. Either go through the canyon, or to wander against the mountains. Maria chose to go through the canyon. The heat from the noonday sun was baking everything as far as the eye could see. As they wandered a few miles leading up to the to the canyon, Jack observed that there was no vegetation at all. The sparse manzanita and cactus and disappeared, the only thing that remained was just some low growing weeds.

As they move closer to the canyon, both Jack and Maria noticed that the horses were becoming skittish and a bit more difficult to control.

"Maria, you have any idea what is upsetting the horses?"

"I gotta tell you Jack, I've never seen anything like this. I've seen some horses get spooked at hearing the rattling of the Western diamondback rattlesnake. But there isn't snake around here."

After two more miles, the horses were acting almost as if they were wild again. Snorting, wild head movements and constantly being spurred to move on. Jack and Maria came to a stop at about a half mile from the entrance to the canyon.

"If you asked me, I'd say these animals did not want to go into that canyon. Maria if you have any suggestions on how to calm these horses down, I'm all ears."

Maria finally put two and two together. Her bad dream and now these horses telling her not to go into this canyon. She had no idea what had transpired there a hundred and fifty years ago. She turned her horse to go back the way they came. Lollipop was grateful and made her exit at a very fast pace. Jack reined in Satan to follow her and he too was appreciative.

In a couple miles from that canyon everything was back to normal. Maria reminded Jack of the dream she had the night before. She apologized for not being more attentive as to what they were trying to accomplish.

"I'm really befuddled as to what took place. I think this is a good time for us to call off this trek. The food and water are at a minimum. The horses are enthusiastic about getting back to the barn. But I think we came close, just a feeling."

Jack and Maria's return trip came within about a half mile of John Castellano. Poor bastard! He had no idea what was ahead of him. John had evidently not seen Jack and Maria turn away. It was getting nigh on to sundown, Jack and Maria decided to pitch camp before it became too dark.

John Castellano followed the signs that Jack and Maria had left as they made their way toward the canyon. He sat back in the saddle rather relaxed. He figured they'd probably camp somewhere up in the canyon. Their camp would be above him, he would have to keep the light of his stove blocked.

The closer John came to the entrance of the canyon the more agitated his horse became. Even his pack mule was skittish. As he came upon the entrance to the canyon the horse was unmanageable and the pack mule pulled the rope loose from John's saddle and beat a galloping retreat the way they came. John tried to bring his horse under control, he was absolutely befuddled by the antics of the animals. He turned his horse around and gave him his head and the horse retreated almost at a gallop. As the sun was going down, John was giving full chase to the pack mule who was by now almost a half mile ahead.

There is not much to tie the horses to, except wrap the lines around some very large rocks. Jack had the saddles off and was currying the horses. He heard some clattering in the distance. And against the horizon he could see this mule moving at a full gallop with whatever materials was strapped to him making a clanking sound. All motion stopped as Jack watched this episode unfold before him. The dark-red sky of sundown showed the mule as a dark silhouette. Approximately a half minute later came another horse and rider, silhouetted against the sky. It looked as though the rider was attempting to catch that lead mule. Jack stood there, his arms draped over the back of Satan and he watched the second rider clattering off into obscurity. Maria looked up from the tent that she was erecting and watched. She and Jack turned to look at each other. Jack just shrugged his shoulders.

This is excursion was like the last trip into the desert. Whatever reason(s), the return trip was always faster. Maria studied the map and she came to the conclusion that they would pass by that same stream of water, but would not have to traverse the footbridge. That was quite a relief for Jack. Sure enough, towards the end of the next day they came across the very deep gully and the pristine water that was far below them. The same procedure as before and the animals were all watered.

About one more day, and they should be back to the outpost. Jack and Maria slid into the tent and both were about to go to sleep in their sleeping bags. Maria was about to turn the Coleman lantern off when she came close to Jack and whispered, "What you did out there was extremely brave. You didn't have a gun or any sort of weapon, but you were willing to defend this camp. I didn't know that chivalry was still alive."

Jack looked into her dark eyes, not sure of exactly what to say. "I didn't really have any kind of plan. Mud wrestling was a choice, but I don't think I would've done very well at that either. But thank you for the compliment."

"Jack, I forgot to tell you some good news. My application has been accepted to the Veterinary School of Medicine at the University of Arizona. I'm going to have to go to Tucson to attend classes there. Oh! I just had a thought. I won't have to wear that disgusting uniform from the diner anymore. This just keeps getting better and better." She turned the light out and slid down into the sleeping bag. Jack could see the big smile across her face.

Chapter 18

Tuesday morning came, and the old routine came along also. Bright and early, Maria was behind the counter at the diner. She spent the 4th of July weekend, treasure hunting with her new friend. She did enjoy riding the horses and camping out in the open. But there were some funny events that she and Jack would have to discuss.

Jack woke up, his backside bit sore but it wasn't as bad as his first excursion into the wild. He showered, dressed and joined his mother at the kitchen table. He had plenty to tell her.

"Well, Mom, I'm getting the hang of riding horses. This last time out, I had an all-black horse named 'Satan.' But he wasn't as difficult as I thought he might be. Maria kept me out of any real difficulty and I was very very grateful."

Over a bowl of cereal and milk, Jack had the revised map and a contour map of the Indian reservation. He tried to correlate their trip from their map to what is publicly printed. Things didn't compute. He remembered that during the trip, Maria kept that rock formation that look like a Mexican sombrero always on the left shoulder. There was no such rock formation indicated on the state map. In addition, there was no indication of the gorge and stream that they crossed. The canyon that gave them such difficulty was non-existent. Jack could see that this could contribute to why the treasure never been found. He will have to confer with Maria to figure out their next course of action.

Late in the afternoon, Jack motored over to Maria's diner. As he walked in the door, he could see the man at the end of the counter. The same man, nursing a cup of coffee and slice of apple pie. Jack sat on a stool closest to the cash register. Maria came out from the kitchen area and saw Jack sitting there. Her dark eyes gave away her emotions. She had a couple of plates and headed to a table. She nodded her head as Jack watched her pass by.

"It's nice to see you, today." She handed Jack the menu and pulled out her pad and pen to take his order.

"I'll just have a slice of apple pie and a cup of coffee. I found a couple of things that don't add up. Could you come by after work and we could look at what I discovered?"

Maria poured cup of coffee and retrieved an already cut slice of apple pie. She placed them in front of Jack, she bent low and whispered, "I have to work through the dinner hour, tonight. It will be getting dark by the time I make it over to your house. Will that be any problem?"

"Not a problem. Also, I'd like you to take a look at some of the older periodicals that my grandfather had accumulated. There might be some useful articles for you to study."

It was after nine when Maria arrived. The blazing sunset had melted on the horizon and stars came out to bid adieu.

She parked her bike near the kitchen door. Rita already had the door open to welcome her. The pitcher full of lemonade and ice cubes sat on the table. Jack called her over to the table to inspect some maps.

"Take a look at these, somebody's being hoodwinked I think." Maria bent over to inspect the maps. There was a roadmap, an all-terrain map, the cowhide map with the markings, and the sheets of paper Scotch taped together reflecting the changes made to the original cowhide map. Jack had put a red mark on the modified map to reflect sombrero mountain. None of the other maps identified sombrero mountain nor did they indicate the location of 'Weavers Needle.'

Maria took a pencil and started to draw a line on their map from Claypool and the Happy Trails outfitter. She crossed over the wiggle that represented the creek and continued in a Northeast fashion. She could only guesstimate where the canyon was located.

She sat there looking from one map to the other. Slowly shaking her head, a small grin appeared. "Jack, with these maps, there is no way on this green earth that anyone is going to have a decent chance of finding the Peralta gold. None of the other maps give any serious markings to any of our geological findings. There was no creek, no canyon and the Sombrero Mountain was missing."

Jack added to that, "And not a damn thing about cougars." Rita looked at both of them, her mouth slightly agape. "Mom, we just happened to see one in the distance. We made sure that it never came to close."

Outside in the dark, the shadow of the workshop concealing the figure, a silhouette was monitoring the conversation with the high gain antenna that was pointed at the open kitchen door. Attached was a small recorder, silently remembering the conversations.

Jack Maria studied all of the maps and they came to the conclusion that they were close to where the Peralta gold had been mined. Maria reminded Jack that the terrain was a bit more forgiving and they could shorten the excursion by taking an all-terrain vehicle (ATV).

"Jack, I think the cost of an ATV is going to be higher than a couple horses. I guess gas is more expensive than hay."

"Darn! I was just getting used to sitting on a saddle for three or four hours straight." Jack had an impish grin on his face.

"Well at least you won't be wearing any of that joint cream when you get home."

Rita interjected, "My God, where did you get that stuff? I have never smelled anything so rancid."

Everybody chuckled. Maria confessed that it wasn't anything that she had done to prepare that concoction. It was an old recipe that her grandfather put together a number of years ago. Jack picked up the rawhide map, rolled it up and put it back into the cardboard cylinder it came in.

"Why don't you go into granddad's old examining room. There are huge stacks of periodicals that he kept. Just go through them and see if any of the articles would interest you. I'm going to take the map back to the old workshop. We're not going to need it anymore." With map in hand, Jack walked out the back door to the workshop. A jiggle of the key, he opened the lock and slid the door open. He flipped a switch for the florescent light and tossed the black cylinder onto the workbench. He closed the door, and pressed the lock closed. On the opposite side of the workshop, peering in through the dirty window, was a figure, observing everything.

Jack scrambled back to the house to see Maria and Rita on the floor with piles of periodicals. Dr. Ezra Mitchell had all of the periodicals separated chronologically and each pile was a particular publication. Too bad! The two women completely destroyed any sense of order.

"Maria, did you find anything that interested you?"

"I found several things, and I haven't even scratched the surface."

"I have an idea. Seeing that there are so many that you are interested in, how about, I just simply bring them all to your apartment and you can decide what's pertinent?"

The periodicals were finally placed in small columns but there was no rhyme or reason to what was in each pile. A deck of cards couldn't have been shuffled more efficiently.

As Maria was leaving by way of the kitchen door, she reminded Jack that she still had to work through the end of the week. She would attempt to swap shifts to get a three-day weekend. If they left straightaway from her job on Friday perhaps, they could get one more excursion to go treasure hunting.

She was on her bike and pedaling down the front driveway. Streetlights lit her way home. The figure in the darkness quietly disassembled his electronic gear. He watched the lights of the house. The back door closed and the kitchen light extinguished. From each end of the house came a glow from bedroom windows. Soon, those lights turned off. Just a matter now to wait for approximately 30 minutes and everyone should be asleep.

Quietly stepping over the rocky ground, that solitary figure came to the locked door of the workshop. With a small penlight flashlight in his mouth, he fumbled through a set of keys and inserted one in the Master lock. With the dexterity of a surgeon, he jiggled the lock and key together. Finally, the lock opened. Great care taken to slowly slide the door open without that creaking sound. The beam from the flashlight illuminated just the workbench. There was the tube, with the rawhide map inside. It was just a second, the map was gone and the door closed. The lock was back on duty. A minuscule crunch of rubber sole shoes across the arid ground. No one would know for days that the map was missing.

Chapter 19

John Castellano had some work to do. First, he had to transcribe the conversations that took place in the kitchen. Second, he had to copy the map. And lastly, he had to share the map with his newfound bar buddy, Billy Watson. Oh yeah, there was a report that he had to fill and send to Mr. William Benton.

The sun rose again in the East, with a fiery determination to melt everything in sight. After breakfast, Jack piled the magazines into the trunk of his car. Far too many to be tied up with a single rope. Categorizing the different issues would keep Maria busy on rainy nights. It was in late afternoon, during the heat of the day, and Jack decided to drive by the diner.

Jack enjoyed going to the diner. He would use the flimsiest of excuses to have a cup of coffee there. Maria was a smart woman, but she didn't need to be told that. She had a way of having people see her side of the situation and they were glad they did. Jack sat at his usual stool next to the cash register. Today was a bit different. Jack noticed that the balding, older man was not at his usual place at the end of the counter.

"Maria, I don't see your guardian here today. You think that his people may have counted everything in that warehouse, finally?"

"Yeah, he was becoming quite a regular in here. He was a quiet enough fellow. It took a while for me to feel comfortable with him constantly watching me."

"I have quite an armload of those periodicals in the trunk of my car. I couldn't find anything to tie them up. What would you like me to do with?"

"Hmm. Let me think a minute. How about, you just put them in the vestibule of my apartment building. I don't think I have to worry about people in the building wanting to know how to 'Deworm' their pet dog. I'll look and see if I can find something to tie all those issues together. Could you give me a lift out to the reservation tomorrow?"

Jack and Maria chatted for about 20 minutes and a couple of customers came in to start the dinner rush. Jack confirmed that he would drop off the magazines to her building. He told her to call him in the morning when she wanted to leave. With that, he left and drove over to Maria's apartment building.

It took Jack about 15 minutes to drive to the apartment building, and another 5 to 6 minutes to schlep the armloads of magazines into the foyer of the building. He drove off contented that he was able to be of help to Maria. About two blocks down the road, at the stoplight, there was a weather-worn marquee announcing that the Road Runner Bar was open for business. Jack noticed, in the front parking lot, there sat that faded pickup truck that Maria had driven to the reservation. Probably her roommate, Billy, was inside. Jack knew that it was too early in the day for a working stiff to be in there and if someone was working swing shift that would not be the place to go beforehand.

Maria did mention that Billy Watson just shared the apartment to rent with her. She wasn't impressed with Billy's work ethic. He had a succession of jobs, none of which lasted very long. His latest achievement was getting fired from a city job. Billy used his Apache heritage to give himself leverage on his job applications. Poor boy, fell into that trap. He liked liquor but it didn't like him. It was common knowledge that everyone knew the American Indian does not have the particular enzyme to metabolize alcohol. It doesn't take much for an Indian to get drunk. In Billy's case, he had to stay sober enough to know where the unemployment office is located.

Jack pulled into an open slot in the parking lot and just for curiosity he went into the bar. The door opened silently and Jack knew he was in a different world. The lights were dim, the overhead fans turned slowly. Dirty windows filtered the sunlight. The stagnant air was a mixture of cigarette smoke, sweat, and cheap alcohol. Jack took a seat at the table near the back wall and let his eyes become accustomed to the reduced lighting. Three or four people were sitting at tables and the same number sitting at the bar. The bartender raised a beer stein in Jack's direction. The thumbs-up from Jack let the bartender know a schooner of beer was what Jack desired. Jack remembered that Billy Watson had his black hair braided coming down his back. Sure enough, there was a kid sitting at the bar who had a long braid. Billy was having a rather animated conversation with the fellow on this stool next to him. Jack squinted his eyes and concentrated, the guy looks familiar. Then it came to him. The fellow sitting next to Billy Watson was the same corpulent man who sat in the diner eating pie and watching Maria Two Crows.

An inner voice told Jack that this was not a coincidence. He quietly sipped his beer and watched the backs of the fellows at the bar. Music from the jukebox made eavesdropping on conversations impossible. Jack thought it was important that those two at the bar did not know he was aware of their association. Quietly, he was out the door, leaving a half glass of beer on the table. He drove back to the diner with the radio off. His mind racing, to find that thread of connection. Nothing came to mind.

John Castellano sat in the bar next to Billy Watson. John fed the boy schooners of beer and just listened. Billy explained that the girl he shared an apartment had written her accounts of some dreams she had growing up. She told her friends that the dreams had something to do with gold. John asked some leading questions that encouraged Billy to lay out his ideas.

"I hunted for that book for several months in the apartment, and I didn't get anywhere. Then a drinking buddy gave me an idea and I took a search of the place she lived on the reservation. I found the book!"

"I've been having a helluva time trying to figure out what she wrote down. She gives description of rock formations that she imagined in the dream. When she wrote down what she remembered from the dream, she never indicated what direction she went. But she did make mention of the moon. I used that to get the general direction."

Jack pulled into the diner parking lot and strode with purpose to his usual seat by the cash register. Not many people in the diner and the early afternoon. Jack scanned them all at the various tables. Nobody else at the counter.

Maria had just finished cleaning coffeepot when Jack came in. With a finger, Jack motioned for Maria to come by.

"Maria, you're not going to believe what I just discovered. I delivered those periodicals to your apartment house. They're lying in loose piles in the corner of the foyer. When I left, I passed an aging saloon about two blocks from your building. Out front, I noticed that beat up pickup truck of your roommate. Out of curiosity, I went inside. I don't know if you've ever been to that particular place, but I got to tell you it's a dump! I sat at a table in the back of the place and watched people. Your roommate was sitting at the bar in a very animated conversation with, you believe this. The guy he was talking to is the fellow was sitting at the end of your counter every day, having a cup of coffee and a piece of pie."

Maria just stood there looking at Jack. She looked down, and there was no one sitting on any of the stools. The apple pie man was absent.

"Maria, I've been racking my brain trying to figure out what the connection is between the two of them. I think they're watching you, but I don't know why. One fellow watches you during the day at work, the other watches you in your apartment. Have you had any conversations with the fellow who comes in for a cup of coffee and piece of pie?"

Maria thought for a moment, and asked Jack if he wanted anything to drink. She was still deep in thought when she brought a glass of iced tea to Jack.

Her head bent over slightly, and she shook it in a negative fashion and told Jack, "I don't think we had much to talk about all. He only mentioned that he was supervising an inventory of a warehouse. I must admit if he just came here on his break, his breaks are couple hours long."

"Let's keep this piece of news under our hat. That I would ask you to be a bit more aware of his actions and maybe dispositions when he comes in here. I just thought of something. When did this fellow first show up at the counter?"

Maria brightened up and smiled. "He was probably the only fellow to order any pie. We've ordered approximately three pies this past month. He showed up about the same time you started coming by. Jack, you think this fellow is watching you also?"

"Could be. But for the life of me I can't figure out what would be important for a fellow to spend his time watching us."

"Jack, I didn't want to say anything to you, but on both of our treks into the outback we were followed."

"How did you know all of that?"

"On the first trip, we were setting up camp the first evening. I saw a glimpse of light reflecting off of a pair of binoculars. Do you remember tying some cloth to the hooves of our animals? I used that as a diversion for whoever was following us. On our second trip, you remember seeing someone galloping after their pack mule a bit after sundown? I think someone is going to let us find the gold and then take it from us?"

Jack looked into Maria's eyes. He didn't say a word. He slid off the stool and paid for his drink. As he got to the entrance of the diner, he turned to Maria and quietly said, "Be very careful out there."

Jack spent his time driving home, deep in thought. He was trying to figure out how anyone would know about the jaunts that he and Maria took into the outback. Rita had dinner on the stove and waiting for him. He spent the dinner time with Rita explaining the things that he had encountered during the day. One of Rita's best qualities was her ability to sit and listen.

"Jack, let's take a look at the things you did once you first found that cylinder. Let's just look at things, one at a time."

Maria finished her shift and bicycled back to her apartment. She carried the bicycle up the steps and into the foyer. Sitting there, was a loose pile of magazines that Jack had delivered earlier. They needed to be stacked tied up. Maria had seen some cord behind the seat of Billy's old pickup. There was the pickup in the usual slot allotted to her apartment.

Maria opened the driver's door to the pickup and tilted the back of the seat forward. There was the cord, the loops were uniform and tied together. Then she saw it, a few inches away. Her body stiffened. It felt as though all her skin was being jabbed by pins. She stood there, staring, unable to grasp what she was looking at. Seconds went by. Gradually, the shock wore off. She reached in to confirm what she saw. There in her shaking hands, was her dream book.

Maria leafed through the pages. Some of them had scribbled notes beside the entries. As the reality set in, rage began to fill her very being. Maria remembered where she had kept the book, in a slot of the bedpost at her grandfather's house. She must've had a million questions racing through her mind. Why was it in the back of Billy Watson's truck? What were the scribblings that he inserted? How long had it been in the truck? What the hell was going on?

She thought about confronting Billy with the book. She knew that in her anger, she might not be thinking correctly. She took the cord out and put the book back. She tied up the bundles of magazines thinking about what her reaction should be.

"I'll go over to Rita and Jack's house."

Out the door and down the steps, Maria pedaled furiously across Apache Junction. Rita answered the doorbell. She opened the door, and in the light from the street lamp stood Maria. Her face glistened with sweat, the underarms of her blouse and down the front with a dark stain.

"Lord girl! You look as though you've been chased by the devil. Come in, and I'll get you something to drink."

Jack was sitting at the kitchen table with a couple of sheets of paper in front of him. He looked up as Maria came to the doorway. Sweat was dripping off of her everywhere "Who came in second at the race?" He smiled and gestured around to have a seat.

"Jack, you won't believe what I just discovered. Do you remember my telling you about a notebook, where I jotted down dreams that I had? Well, I found that notebook and it was in the back of Billy Watson's old pickup truck. He had to have stolen it from my grandfather's house. I am so damned angry, I could commit mayhem on that little bastard!" She sat heavily on the kitchen chair. Maria's energy level was high and she needed something to do with her hands. Absent mindedly, she grabbed her long braid and proceeded to undo the plait.

"Just exactly what was in your dream book? Billy Watson doesn't impress me as some sort of fellow to be very conniving. Although we had two incidents happen today and there he is, in the middle of both of them."

"Jack, you mentioned this afternoon that you had seen Billy Watson with the fellow who sits in my diner with pie and coffee. That man never came in today. Now I find my dream book in the back of Billy Watson's truck. What do you think the connection is?"

Jack thought for a moment, "That man watches you when you're working in the diner. Billy Watson keeps tabs on you when you're in your apartment. The only time when you are free is when we take a trek out into the hinterland. And you reminded me that both times we were out, we were followed. I don't know how much closer to our vest we can keep our cards."

Maria sat there and listened. "I have an idea," she said. "Let's take one last trip, but this time let's use an all-terrain vehicle. It will be damned difficult for them to keep up with us if we have an ATV and they're on horseback. Besides, an ATV will shorten our time in the outback. Also, cougars don't usually attack machines."

Jack got a slight smirk. "If we take horsemeat off the cat's menu, what other prey you think comes to the top of the list?"

"Jack, I've tied up the batches of magazine. Could you give me a lift tomorrow morning to the reservation? We can take the magazines there and I can snoop around and find out if anybody is watching us. I have to go back to the apartment. Take a shower, change clothes and get things together. I just hope I can keep my mouth shut and not tip Billy off to him know that I am aware of what he has done."

"I'll pick you up about 8 o'clock, before the sun heats everything up. Can you put a reservation into the outfitters store for some supplies and the ATV? We'll use my credit card."

Maria left out the kitchen door. In her agitated disposition, she made it back to the apartment in record time. Up the flights of stairs and into the apartment she carried her 10-speed bike. There was Billy, laying on the couch and watching television. Salutations exchanged,

Mary was working really hard to keep her voice normal. She mentioned that Jack Cummings was going to take her out to the reservation, hauling some magazines connected with veterinary science. A disinterested, "humph" was the only response as Billy searched through the channels.

Chapter 20

The next morning was an imitation of the previous day. The sun came up like thunder and promised to scorch everything on earth. Maria spent her time talking to the salesperson at Happy Trails Outfitter's. She had the requirements memorized and changed the transportation from horseback to an all-terrain vehicle. She wasn't sure how far they'd be going, so she asked for an extra five-gallon can of gasoline.

Jack pulled up and Maria put several bundles of magazines into the trunk. They quickly left the town behind and headed down the highway on US-60 then on into US-70. Jack brought along a couple bottles of chilled water. Maria twisted off the cap of one bottle, and as she let the cool liquid embrace her tongue she thought, "What a nice gesture."

It took Jack almost 2 hours to drive into San Carlos. He slowed down and took directions from Maria to navigate through the dusty roads. They pulled up next to the building that held the examination table and other medical instruments. The door was slightly ajar. The door opened with a slight squeak. There was hardly any furniture in the place, so Maria had no trouble finding space for the magazines and periodicals. Jack and Maria each had bundles of magazines.

"Let's go talk to my grandpa while we're here. Maybe I'll get a couple of hints on who was following us."

As they pulled up to the little bungalow they could see the old man in the backyard, sitting in a chair. He rested his gnarled hands on each knee. Charlie "Red Fox" was concentrating on something on the distant horizon. He didn't hear Maria come into the yard. Maria called his name and touched his shoulder. Charlie Red Fox visibly jumped at being recalled back to the present.

"Sichoo, I'm so sorry for having disturbed you. Are you okay? Jack and I brought by some publications that explain different problems that animals may have. When I have some time off, I'll be going through these to help hone my skills."

Charlie slumped slightly in his chair, reached out and patted Maria's arm. "I was daydreaming. I was remembering times long ago when 'shinálí,' your grandmother, was here."

"Sichoo, let's go inside. Jack and I brought some cool water. We all can talk and sip some refreshing water."

The house was actually cooler than outside. The sunlight was greatly reduced. When Jack entered, it felt a little bit like entering a cave. All three sat around the kitchen table and Maria served the bottles of chilled water. Maria made small talk of things she noticed going on around the reservation. She asked her grandfather if Billy Watson had come to visit. Charlie mentioned that the boy came by looking for a charm that might help him when he was looking for another job.

Charlie took a long swig from the bottle of water and then rubbed his hands. "Are you still looking for that treasure of gold? With the sun being so hot this time of year, I would imagine it would be very difficult to go exploring."

"Mr. Morgan, your granddaughter is quite at home in the desert. She's taught me a lot on how to survive under these sultry conditions. We haven't found anything positive but were going to give it one more try at the end of this week."

"We're not sure what the size of the treasure would be, but if it turns out to be substantial, what do you think your tribe will do with the findings?"

Charlie took his time thinking about the question. Slowly he rubbed his hands together deep in thought. "I'm not sure what the exact determination will be, but consensus is to build a casino."

Maria seemed a bit concerned about her grandfather's answer. "A casino? Streets needed to be paved. The water pipes were 100 years old and nothing comes out now but rust water. There could be a decent school built on the reservation. And your first priority is… A casino!"

Charlie didn't respond. He sat there slowly rubbing his hands and when Maria had finished, Charlie's only response was to shrug his shoulders.

Maria thought it was better to change the subject. "In your wanderings about the reservation and council meetings has anyone ever expressed interest in what Jack and I were doing? We've been followed on a couple of our trips into the desert. We were gone for several days on each trip. For someone to shadow us for those days, would tell me they were willing to spend money and time."

Charlie sat there at the table, he took several drinks of water from the bottle. Then shook his head slightly side to side. He couldn't think of anyone on the reservation who had the time, money, or interest to have Maria watched.

Charlie mentioned that his two-burner stove no longer worked. He asked Maria if she and Jack could take a look and see what the problem was. Maria went to the stove lit a match then turned on the stove. She watched but there was no flame to ignite. Jack peaked around the back and saw a small copper pipe going around the floor and out a hole in the wall. He took a look outside and there was the copper pipe going over to a propane tank. Jack looked at the gauge on the tank. Empty!

"Maria, this is an easy fix. Call the propane company and have them deliver a fresh tank to your grandfather's house." Maria was about to call the gas company when suddenly she had an idea. She went outside to get the size of the canister. It was a large tank that laid horizontally on a small cradle. She went over and saw that the logo said the canister was 1000 lbs. Maria called the gas company and gave them Charlie Red Fox's address. When she asked them what the price would be, her eyebrows squinted together and serious expression came on her face.

"Jack I think there's a problem. They gave me a quote of $300. I don't think grandfather has that kind of money and neither do I. Is there anything you can do to help?"

Jack took the receiver of the phone and talked to the gas company representative. He made sure they were aware of the address and impressed on them the need to have the tank filled by tomorrow. He had the expense added to his credit card and waved Maria away from the phone when she wanted to make some comments.

"Charlie," Jack held Charlie's hand to get his attention. "Tomorrow, there will be a deliveryman coming to your home and he is going to fill the tank that's in the back of your house with gas. This gas will go to your stove and it'll start working again. Ask the man if he could do a quick check to ensure there are no leaks."

Charlie smiled and took his both hands to shake Jack's. His head nodded a couple of times. "I guess I'm becoming forgetful. I had forgotten that the stove was connected to that tank."

Maria made some comments and told her grandfather that she would be into visit him a lot more often. And that these little problems would go away. She gave the old man kiss and a very warm hug and told him she would return in couple days.

Jack shook Charlie's hand and bid him good fortune. The old man saw the pouch hanging around Jack's neck. A smile came to Charlie's face and he lightly tapped Jack's chest. "You are a very smart man to heed my words. There are strange things happening on our land."

Jack and Maria sat for some time not talking as Jack sped down the highway back to Apache Junction. Maria turned and watched Jack for some time as he drove. Finally, she said, "That was one of the nicest things you could do. Since we've been on this quest, I've found out some things about you. You don't take yourself too seriously, you're open to learning new things, you have great respect for women, you're brave, and you have great respect for elders. Jack you have only one flaw in your makeup. You're not an Apache. Darn it!"

Jack sat and listened to what Maria was saying. At the end, he got very embarrassed and his cheeks grew red. Maria watched in a broad smile came across her face. "Jack, I do believe you are embarrassed."

"No, I'm not embarrassed. I was taking your hint. I was trying to become a 'red man' just like you had asked." Both Jack and Maria laughed out loud. They both felt really good.

The ride home gave Jack and Maria the opportunity to discuss what they wanted to accomplish on this last trek into the outback. Maria said that they could take an ATV and retrace their previous steps. She said that if they moved East leaving the outfitter's store, they would be able to move around that creek and the footbridge completely. Jack expressed concern of running out of gas while they were out. He suggested an extra 5 gallon can of gas tied to the back of the ATV. Maria asked him if he had any particular desires for food. She reasoned that with an ATV you could put more on it than on a pack mule. Jack suggested a can of Spam would be nice addition. Maria just looked at him like he had two heads. The last trip covered terrain that had very little vegetation. They both agreed that a small cookstove with a propane bottle attached would be ideal. It was Maria's work schedule that determined when they should go. The choices were, to go tomorrow or wait a couple of days when Maria was scheduled off. Jack was very wary of doing things with little planning. When he was much younger, his impetuosity led to some terrible outcomes.

After a little thought, Jack decided he would use the time to do a little sightseeing about the Phoenix area. Maria made several suggestions that would keep him occupied. There was an abandoned settlement called "Goldfield" it was now a tourist attraction. He could go on down the road and take some pictures of "Weavers Needle." Farther down that same road was an old-time generals store/bar. What made the place so unique was that people would take dollar bills, sign their name and date to it and the establishment would staple it to the walls. The entire place, the walls, lampshades, were covered, with autographed dollar bills. It's said that there was approximately $200,000 on the walls. And when you sat at the bar you did not have a stool to sit on. You had a western saddle! The name of this place was called, "Tortilla Flat."

Chapter 21

The days passed quickly. Jack took his mother, Rita, to go along with him. All the time that she had been taking care of her father there was no opportunity for Rita to have any time to relax. They visited the Cactus Garden and some so many different cactus specimens. Every plant had spines on the growths. One of the tall Saguaro cactus had a hole in one of the arms about eight or 9 feet off the ground. Some small species of owl had made a nest in the cactus.

When they visited Goldfield, they were treated with a visit into the gold rush days. All the buildings were roughhewn wood and beaten by the blazing sun. Trinket shops now took over storefronts. You could even tour the local whorehouse from the 1850s. The ladies of ill-repute back then were shunned by the rest of the women of the town. But it was these shunned women who paid for the building of the school and even contributed to the church. It seems that back in those days, size did matter. The most profitable women were the ones who were of ample size.

Women who were broad in the beam were more desirable to the men working in the gold fields. There was still an old-time bar open at the end of the dirt street to satisfy a thirst. Most of the libations came from a bottle, even if you ordered a "sarsaparilla."

Jack and Rita took a drive north and visited the town of Sedona. The rock formations all around the town left Rita speechless. As they wandered the different shops, Rita came to the conclusion that the town was populated by artisans. Jewelry from turquoise to black opals abound the different shops. Jack bought several pieces and even got himself a bolo tie with a large polished turquoise stone set in silver. Rita reminded Jack that any man who was courageous enough to wear a turquoise bolo tie, needed to have an audacious turquoise ring. It just so happened that Rita was looking into a display case that had audacious turquoise rings.

Jack pulled into the diner about an hour before the end of Maria's shift. At the end of the counter was the same fellow nursing a cup of coffee. Jack had decided that it was best to leave the fellow undisturbed. If John Castellano knew that Jack and Maria were aware of his true reason of being in the diner, nothing was ever said. The game just continued. Jack asked Maria to write down a list of things to take on this trip.

"Maria, have you ever used an ATV on any of your trips to the back country? Does the outfitter need a couple of days of advance notice to put this all together?"

"I never used an ATV myself, but I've seen a number of people take them on trips to the outback."

It didn't take Maria long to make at the list. She had done this a couple of times over the past few weeks. She made a second list to remind Jack of the personals that he wanted to bring along. Toothpaste, toothbrush, underwear and maybe some socks.

Jack phoned in the requirements to the outfitters store right from the counter of Maria's diner. He made a point of requesting an ATV for this trip. He told the fellow that only two people would be on this trip. His last request was for an extra 5 gallon can of gasoline. The bill was $200 higher than the previous excursion. Jack thought for a moment and decided the extra expense versus feeding and watering the horses, plus the saddles, not to mention the vile salve was just perfect.

"Maria, there are some things I have to take care of home. How about I come by your apartment in say, two hours? You have your stuff for the trip packed, and I'll take you over to my grandfather's house. You can spend the night in the spare bedroom. Tomorrow, we'll be able to get an early start." Maria thought that was an excellent idea and nodded her head in agreement.

The fellow at the end of the counter contentedly sipped his coffee. His nonchalant attitude was a façade. His ears drinking every morsel of the conversation by the cash register. John Castellano had taken several trips into the desert. He and the fellow who ran the outfitters store had come to an understanding. John just told the outfitter how long he would be in the desert and any special requirements. John's expense account paid handsomely. The outfitter knew that John shadowed various expeditions. For the increased business, the outfitter never mentioned a word.

John thought for a moment, and decided it was time to include Billy Watson in the plan. He had looked over that rawhide map that he had stolen from the workshop. He found it impossible to decipher what any of the symbols were. Perhaps if he showed it to the young Watson boy, they might be able to decipher it.

No sense being in a hurry, after all, the people he was trailing were sitting in the diner. He took his time with the coffee and read a bit of a newspaper left on the counter. The Cummings boy paid his bill and left. A couple of more minutes was wasted on reading someone's account of the rodeo that had occurred over 4th of July holiday. Casual saunter out the door, John knew exactly where to go. 15 minutes later, it was in the parking lot of the Road Runner bar. There at the other end of the parking lot was Billy Watson's beat up old pickup truck. Before he went in, John retrieved the rolled-up cowhide map the trunk.

Billy Watson was sitting at the bar with a couple of empty Budweiser bottles keeping him company. John tapped him on his shoulders he went past and pointed to a table in the very of the bar. The map was rolled out by the time Billy sat down at the table.

"I got this from a workshop behind Maria's boyfriends house. Do you recognize any of the markings on this map?" Billy's fingers traced over some of the markings burned into the cowhide. He looked closely at the map. He rose up, shaking his head from side to side.

"We have a copy of this map the Apache Museum. That old woman who tended to Herman Weiss was making copies of this map and selling them. Nobody has come close to finding the mine."

Billy and John sat at the table, just staring at the map. John Castellano had followed several people out into the desert who were looking for the gold. None of them ever went in the direction that Maria and Jack took that last time they went out. Billy went out to his pickup, tossed the backrest forward and retrieved Maria's dream book. Both he and John reviewed each of the dreams that Maria had annotated. Billy had scribbled some notes beside each of the dreams.

"From the things that Maria listed in her dreams, I believe we will have a good shot at getting the gold. I suspect we'll be looking North to Northeast."

"That was the general direction that those two headed the last time they went out. But I ran into something that I had no control. Both my horse and pack mule were so spooked that I had to call it quits. I heard the fellow make arrangements over the phone for another trek that I expect to start tomorrow. This time I overheard him reserve an ATV. I think if I follow him on horseback I wouldn't be able to keep up."

Billy asked John what the terrain was like during his trip. If there were not too many gullies, maybe they could use Billy's old pickup. John picked up on Billy's comment. He had included both of them on the trip. John said that he wasn't sure of when Jack and Maria were going to start their trip, but he guessed it would be in the early morning. John made his call to the outfitter store and requisitioned enough supplies for two men to last three days. He also pointed out that he would not need any horses. He asked the outfitter how soon he could pick up the gear. The fellow at the store said that without horses or any other transportation involved, he could pick the material up in as early as two hours. John said that he would be over to the outfitters store in about an hour or so. The timing was perfect. He told Billy that he had some errands to run. As he was leaving the bar, John mentioned over his shoulder, "Have your personal stuff in a rucksack, your truck all gassed and oiled, and I'll be by at sunup."

Chapter 22

Maria finished her shift as the supper crowd started to come in. She waved to the girl relieving her and said that she would see her and about three or four days. The anticipation of this trip was a source of excitement for her. As she pedaled her bicycle back to the apartment, she tried to figure out the cause for the excitement. Did she really think they would find the gold? She did enjoy Jack's company. He was a handsome fellow with a mischievous wit. He had no difficulties in taking directions and it didn't bother him to take directions from a woman. The more she thought about him, the warmer it made her feel. There was one last thought that brought a smile to her face, he smelled good.

Jack came by just as the sun was going down. Another really hot day was drawing to a close. Rita had just pulled the steaks off the grill as Jack and Maria arrived. It had been a long while since Rita had any meals served on the back deck. As she put the baked potatoes into a covered bowl, she wondered, if Jack and Maria would be a "item." She promised herself not to be very aggressive as a matchmaker. The salad tossed, and the rest of the table set, Rita surveyed the setting. One last task before calling to dinner. She retrieved an old boombox and put the CD of "cocktail music."

"Time for dinner, everyone!" Jack had just finished putting Maria's tote sack in the spare bedroom. They both appeared at the kitchen door, and saw what Rita prepared. Everyone had a nice smile. Jack and Maria responded to the sight of the upcoming meal, and Rita was smiling at the possibility of a romance.

The sun gave up the sky with a flourish. All along the horizon, reds and oranges mixed together, eventually merging into the indigo of the night. Jack was a bit quiet over his meal, but Rita and Maria kept conversation going with all sorts of discussions. The citronella candles placed about the patio acted as nightlights.

When they were all seated, Rita recited a prayer for before meals. All heads bowed, both Jack and Maria echoed the same prayer. As Jack passed the baked potatoes, he wondered what religion Maria Two Crows practiced. Surprisingly, throughout the dinner little was mentioned about the upcoming trip into the outback. Jack enjoyed his steak to be medium rare. That is, the steak should leave a small trickle of blood on the plate. A gallon of iced tea with a dozen or so ice cubes was passed around. One of Rita's favorite vegetables was asparagus. Each person at the table had a small bundle of steamed asparagus. The bright green color was topped with a pat of melting butter. Rita had placed a small bouquet of flowers on the center of the table. Either side of the bouquet was a cut glass hurricane candle. Each of the lit candles provided a warm glow over the table. Jack thought the table setting looked very nice, but Rita and Maria had appraised the table sitting quite differently. They both had a Mona Lisa smile as they ate dinner.

When dinner was over by several minutes, Rita collected all of the dishware and took it inside. Maria offered to help, but Rita said there weren't very many dishes and she had a dishwasher, that help wasn't needed. On the way inside, with some dishes, Rita increased the volume of the boombox slightly. Jack sat beside the table looking up to a star-studded sky. They just finished a delicious meal, romantic music is filling the air, and a beautiful young woman was sitting beside him. Gen. Custer had better chance of evasion than Jack did.

Maria sipped her iced tea. She could see that Jack needed a bit of encouragement. She stood up, walked around the table and extended her hand out to Jack. "Come dance with me."

Jack sat there a bit puzzled. He looked from her hand to her eyes and back to her hand again. "I thought you been on your feet all day and were tired."

Maria wiggled her fingers a bit and giggled, "Don't be silly. I'm an Apache Indian woman. We can run for miles, and are noted for our endurance." The Mona Lisa smile was back as she looked down at Jack.

Jack rose and took her into his arms. They swayed slowly around the patio keeping in rhythm with an old song. Rita looked out through the kitchen window and she was smiling broadly. Jack and Maria danced to a couple of songs. Maria noticed that even though Jack's hands and forearms were sinewy hard, his touch around her waist was very gentle. When they were dancing cheek to cheek, Jack could not see Maria's face. And she was smiling broadly also. Jack smelled really good.

Chapter 23

Jack was up at 5 o'clock. While outwardly he didn't show any emotions, the tension inside was building. He showered and made a special effort to get rid of aftershave and any other scents. He heard somewhere that insects are attracted any fragrances or smells that the human body may emit. As Jack was pulling on his beat-up boots, he wondered, "Does Maria have any scents?"

Jack wandered into the kitchen and he could smell the fresh coffee brewing. He hoped that insects wouldn't be attracted to the aroma of coffee. Rita was scurrying about to get breakfast on the table. Maria came in from the spare room, lugging a large knapsack. She had her black hair braided into one large ponytail.

Jack sat at the kitchen table sipping some coffee. He noticed Marie was rather animated in her movements. She was buttering a piece of toast and her hand movements were very jerky. "Maria, are you a bit nervous today?"

"I've had some bad dreams last night. I thought I was over this." Jack reached over and held her hand. Maria sat there and was very appreciative of body contact with Jack. He put her other hand the on top of his and took a deep breath.

"We get on the road and are active, I think that will work this tension and apprehension out of our body." Jack withdrew his hands back from Maria's and he could see melted butter on his fingers. He looked at his hands Maria looked at his hands. They both laughed.

By the time they hit the road, it was light out. It was better than an hour drive to the outfitters store. Maria studied their homemade map. Someone had taken a red felt tip pen and sketched in the two previous trips they had taken.

When Maria concentrated on something she would squint and her eyebrows would narrow together leaving a pair of lines. "I think if we go East for the first day of our trip and then go North we'll be able to avoid that footbridge."

When Jack and Maria arrived, all the gear was stored in the bed of a Polaris 2000 all-terrain vehicle (ATV). It looked pretty sturdy, but there were a few nicks and dings indicating that it had been out before. It had a faded red paint job, a pair of headlights and closed in cab.

Maria went inside with her checklist and confirmed with the manager that those things had been included in her outfit. She had motioned for Jack to come in. He presented the credit card as he looked down Maria's checklist. It was a couple hundred dollars higher than the previous trips. Jack remembered an old saying that his father used to give him when his car broke down. "Get a horse; it's cheaper!"

The outfitter cautioned them to take it a lot slower on terrain that a lot of loose rock. First if there was any slope the vehicle would tend to slide and also loose stones would dig in to the tread of the tires.

With all the gear tied down, Jack slid in behind the wheel and Maria was shotgun. Jack pointed the vehicle into the rising sun. The first couple miles Jack drove rather fast. He and Maria bounced around in the seat like popcorn being made. With a little experimentation, Jack found that driving between ten to 4 ship fifteen mph was much friendlier to the occupants.

Billy Watson and John Castellano sat in Billy's truck some distance away from the outfitters store. Billy had the dream book and John had the rawhide map. There was no need to have a close tail on the two kids. About three hours lapsed before Billy turned the engine over. They stopped at the 7-Eleven store, bought a couple of bags of ice and some quart bottles of water. It more than filled the cooler in the bed of the truck.

By the end of the first day, Jack and Maria had driven approximately even with the location of the footbridge they encountered the previous trip. Ambling through the wide open spaces, wherever you stopped the ATV, was an okay place to set up camp. Maria pulled out the bundle that contained the tent. This was a different kind of setup that utilized the ATV. There was a pole that was inserted vertically into the front bumper and one that was attached vertically at the end of the bed. Maria set out the tarp. The tarp attached to the two vertical poles and made a lean-to. The front and back zipped closed. There was even a little plastic window to look out the front. Maria stood back and admired her work.

Jack found the small propane stove and set it up on the tailgate of the ATV. He took some sausage links from the cooler and put them in the skillet. He added some water to instant mashed potatoes. He was rather proud of himself for having "bangers and mash" out on the trail. Not many places on the ground to sit comfortably, so the tailgate served double duty as table and chairs. Stars started to appear in the night sky. When dinner was done, Maria took some water put it in the skillet, turned on on the propane stove. When it started boiling she scrubbed the skillet clean and then poured the water into the pan used for mashed potatoes. She brought it backup to boiling again and repeated the cleaning process. Jack cut up the plastic plates and put those in a makeshift garbage bag.

Both stood at the entrance of the tent and surveyed the work. Jack noticed a small window and commented, "It's a good thing we have window. Now we can see that cougar when it's coming at us."

"No need to worry Jack, there's a zipper that closes the front door. And you know, cougars don't have opposable thumbs."

"Yep! You're right. Instead of the thumb, he's got a paw full of claws. Hmm. Paws? Claws?. It rhymes. What do ya know. I'm a poet and don't know it, but my feet show it… They're Longfellows." Jack had this goofy looking grin on his face. Maria stood there looking straight at him, her face absolutely deadpan. Jack leaned closer to her as he was preparing to go into the tent. "Well… I thought it was funny."

About a mile or so away, Billy Watson and John Castellano were mimicking same actions as the couple they were following. Billy had turned the truck so it was facing away from their line of travel. With just the parking lights on, they had enough light to finish a couple of ham sandwiches. With two people working, it didn't take hardly any time to erect the pup tent. You can get two people into the tent, but not much else.

Sunup the next morning was like so many before. A cloudless sky whispered hello. The sun rose over the

Superstition Mountains with a crescendo, announcing to the world that it planned to burn everything in the land. Jack and Maria arose at the first light. Maria decided that a couple of pop-tarts would suffice for breakfast. Breaking camp was a lot easier than the previous outings. Jack wasn't sure exactly what he was gaining. But the thought of not having to clean, curry, feed, saddle, and water a horse was a definite positive.

Everything stowed, Jack and Maria sat in the ATV looking at the map. Both were aware of the canyon that had disrupted their last trip. Maria suggested that they move in a more North-Easterly direction. The quiet of the early morning was disturbed by the bellowing of the ATV as it sprang to life.

The boys following behind were just as efficient. While John took down the tent and folded it together, Billy had about pint of water in the in the pan. The propane burner sprang to life and a half handful of ground coffee thrown into the pan would be the start of "Navy coffee."

As the sun grew high in the sky, Maria and Jack worked around the canyon. They kept about a mile from it and did not experience any unusual events. The general terrain of the land was an uphill track. Vegetation was nonexistent. Surface rock had a lot of loose pieces. Jack heeded the admonition of the fellow at the outfitter's store. He slowed the vehicle down and was doing approximately 5 to 10 mile an hour. As he drove around a large outcropping of rock, the terrain flattened out and there was a large mesa.

As Jack slowly drove onto the flat terrain, Maria was looking at the mountains around her. Suddenly things came into focus. She pounded Jack on the shoulder and told him, "Stop! Stop this damn thing now!" Jack slammed on the brakes and brought the vehicle to a halt. He had no idea what Maria had in mind.

"What is your problem? Is this where you want to camp for the night? We still have a lot of afternoon sun left."

"Jack, I've been having some unsettling dreams. I recognize the rock formations that I saw when I was a teenager. The past couple of nights the same formations have upset me."

Maria got out of the ATV and stood beside it. She looked back at the way they had come and she slowly inspected all of the rock formations that surrounded her. She had this feeling. All the things that she had experienced as a child coming into puberty, all of the dreams that woke her up in a sweat was pointing to this place. Her muscles tensed and she needed to hang on the ATV for her balance. Even though her hands held tightly onto the bars of the ATV, her arms shook. She thought she was becoming lightheaded.

With Billy driving the pickup truck and John navigating, they made excellent time. As they drove around the outcropping of rock, they saw Jack and Maria's ATV and it was stopped in the middle of flat open area. Billy slammed on the brakes and the vehicle skidded a bit. Everyone was surprised at the encounter. Four sets of eyes stared at each other in the glaring heat.

Billy was the first to react. "John, the mine is somewhere close to us. I studied the entries in the dream book and did some calculations. We are damn close to the mine. I think I'll put a little scare into her."

Billy tramped on the gas and the wheels shot spray a small rocks behind them. Billy started circling the ATV about 20 yards around. As he picked up speed the circle got larger. There was no let up on the gas pedal. As he drove around

Maria and Jack, a wicked grin spread across his face. His eyes narrowed as the sun shone directly into the windshield.

"We got 'em now, John. We have no need to hide anything, we're in charge now." Billy held Maria's dream book and waved it high. John had picked up on the excitement and he was ecstatic. He waved the cylinder that contained the rawhide map. The pickup truck was now hitting 50 miles an hour and kicking up a rooster tail of dust and loose rocks. John waved the cylinder with the map out the window, taunting Jack and Maria.

Jack and Maria watched all of this with a fascination, transfixed. The two maniacs circling about them, wheels grinding, kicking up dust and stones. Billy was making a second circle around the couple, when it happened.

As Billy was driving around , the bright sun, came shining through the bug- stained windshield. He didn't see any changes in the landscape. There beyond him, was the edge of a cliff. The ground dropped away to about 100 feet down. The edge of the cliff blended in with the rest of the terrain. It was impossible to see until you were upon it. As they drove off the edge, there was that split-second when they became aware of their awful predicament.

The pickup truck for about a tenth of a second, hung out in space, the forces had yet begun to claim their mistake. Billy's eyes opened wide as terror seeped into his reality. One hand holding the damning dream book, the other hand on the steering wheel that turned freely. John turned to him for an explanation as the first sense of weightlessness arrived. The next few seconds would give the most complete answer. But no one would be alive to grasp it.

The pickup nozed down and the front wheels touched the wall of the cliff. That was enough to start the cartwheel down the last 75 feet of nothingness. The truck made two complete revolutions and while in the air, the entire contents of the bed was strewn haphazardly. The truck landed at the bottom of the cliff. The front of the truck stabbed heavily into the unforgiving rocks. The final resting place was on three wheels but the fourth bent at an angle, was turning freely. It was this final stop that proved fatal.

The truck cascaded over the cliff and made it to the bottom without catching fire. No equipment was left in the bed of the truck but two victims remained in the cab. John Castellano died instantly when his skull hit the frame around the windshield. Billy got a last wish. While being thrown about and the intense stop of the truck at the bottom of the cliff, Billy's neck was broken. His head, hung at an unnatural angle. Billy's last view thru the empty windshield, was of white parched bones, of the gold laden mules of Miguel Peralta. The sacks torn and disintegrating, countless blocks of pure gold strewn through the brush. Unable to breathe, Billy Watson's last thought on earth was, the treasure of the Peralta's.

As Maria watched the truck slide out of sight over the cliff, she screamed. Jack just stood there. He couldn't speak, he couldn't move. The whole scenario played out in less than a minute. Now, as they both stood transfixed, gazing at the cliff, a silence creeped across the mesa. Curiosity urged both of them to look over the edge. Before this, no one had any idea of the danger so eminent. With small steps they approach the edge, afraid of the beast that awaited them.

The view to the bottom brought mixed emotions. The truck stood out distinctly among the sea of white bones and glittering gold. Jack and Maria stood at the edge a long time. Eventually, the solemnity of the view began to fade. Jack and Maria held hands as they stood there. Finally they sat down, their legs hanging over the edge. Any emotion that they might have felt, drained away.

"You think anyone's alive down there? I'm surprised that the truck hasn't burst into flames."

"That sure is a long way down, and I don't see any easy way to climb down the cliff face. Do we have any rope long enough to to reach the bottom?"

As they sat there, attentions turned to the gold bricks strewn about the canyon floor. The gold had been laying out in the weather for over 150 years and had not tarnished one iota. Maria was the first to bring up the subject of courting the gold back to civilization.

"If we take all of this back, the council will want 70% of what we find. From our conversation with grandpa, the council plans to build a casino on reservation land. Our people are poor, and the council wants to bring gambling, drinking, prostitution and maybe some connection with organized crime. Jack I don't have a very good feeling about this."

"I know what you mean Maria, I don't have good feelings about this either. I know darn well that the IRS will be looking for their share. Considering what the federal government perpetrated on the American Indian over the years, I don't think that they should get any of this. Here's something that we may have not thought. When this gold was first mined, a lot of people were killed. Over the years, people have been going out into the desert looking for the Peralta gold. And quite a few have not returned. The two fellows who caught up with us today are dead. I think the gold is cursed."

They both sat there for a long time looking down into the canyon. Each recognized that they have the power to change their life and possibly the lives of many other people.

"You know Jack, I'll be attending University of Arizona's School of Veterinary Medicine come this fall. One of those bricks of gold would go a very long way towards my schooling."

"Maria, I see the temptation. But you know, you can't do that. You sell one brick, just one. People are going to be asking questions. Do you want to lie to them? If you tell them the truth, you'll have a casino in your town. I think it comes down to this. We either take all of the gold or we take nothing and tell everyone we didn't find anything."

Maria got up and slowly walked back to the ATV. She climbed into the passenger seat and sat there for a while. Jack followed behind and he climbed into the driver's seat. Jack reached into the cooler for a bottle of water. After a healthy drink, he offered it over to Maria. She looked Jack straight in the eye. "Dammit! Let me ask you, is there anything that gold would accomplish for you?"

Jack shrugged his shoulders and had sort of a rye smile on his face. "Maria, I found my Apache gold!" He knew exactly the dilemma that Maria was fighting. You can ask for help solving a problem, but when it comes down to the end, only you can make the decision.

Maria moved a bit closer, "Jack, I want you to do two things for me."

"If I can be of any help, just ask."

"Right now I want you to kiss me. Then when we get back to town, I want you to take me to the best restaurant in town. I want to put all this behind us and have a marvelous time together. Let somebody else make the decision on what to do with the Apache gold."

The following websites have been helpful in the writing of this story and may provide more information to readers who are interested.

http://americanindianoriginals.com/a
http://americanindianoriginals.com/Native-American-Culture.html
https://www.everyculture.com/North-America/Western-Apache-Religion-
    and-Expressive-Culture.html
http://www.ancientfacts.net/about/apache-indians/
https://en.wikipedia.org/wiki/Peralta_massacre
https://allthatsinteresting.com/lost-dutchman-mine
https://en.wikipedia.org/wiki/Lost_Dutchman%27s_Gold_Mine
http://www.thelostdutchmangoldmine.com/lost-dutchman/4/

CPSIA information can be obtained
at www.ICGtesting.com
Printed in the USA
BVHW012014270921
617439BV00011B/14